Unexpected Ride

A Dark Mafia Romance

Never Been Caught 1

By Ivy Wonder

Published in United States by:

Ivy Wonder

© Copyright 2020 – Ivy Wonder

ISBN-13: 978-1-64808-011-1

ALL RIGHTS RESERVED. No part of this publication may be reproduced or transmitted in any form whatsoever, electronic, or mechanical, including photocopying, recording, or by any informational storage or retrieval system without express written, dated and signed permission from the author.

Table of Contents

Synopsis 1
Prologue 2
Chapter 1 6
Chapter 2 15
Chapter 3 23
Chapter 4 28
Chapter 5 36
Chapter 6 43
Chapter 7 50
Chapter 8 57
Chapter 9 69
Chapter 10 83
Chapter 11 90
Chapter 12 95
Chapter 13 103
Chapter 14 109
Chapter 15 118
Chapter 16 124
Epilogue 128

Synopsis

A desperate woman running from her abusive mobster father gets unintentionally rescued when the car she's fettered in is stolen by a witty car thief. When he discovers her trussed up in the trunk, she offers her inadvertent hero a quarter million in jewels for a ride out of her father's territory. With her father's men and a determined FBI agent on their tail, the pair makes a run for the Canadian border...while the heat between them threatens to be a lethal distraction.

Blurb
I jacked a car tonight with a bound woman in the trunk.
Looks like I saved her life—isn't that ironic?
Now she's offering me a pile of jewels to get her to Montreal.
I take the job to get a chance at taking her.
Those first few nights are hot—but she's got a secret.
She's the mob boss's daughter—and he wants her back.
I haven't had a woman this amazing in my entire life.
I'll drive like the devil to keep her safe.
But with both the mob and the FBI after us, do we have a chance of a clean getaway?

Prologue
Carolyn

Date: December 29, 2018
Location: Lloyd, New York, 1.5 hours outside of New York City
Subject: Alan Chase
Criminal Record: Sealed Juvenile Record. No adult record. Suspected in 34 separate grand theft auto cases in New York, New Jersey, and Connecticut. Routinely dismissed due to lack of evidence. Subject has never been successfully detained or incarcerated.

I sit back from my laptop screen and stretch, my back popping. I'm stiff from driving and sick of bad weather. It's only an hour and a half from the New York field office on a good day, but I just spent three hours bumper to bumper on 9W in the pouring rain.

I'm here because my boss hates me—the talented and ambitious new transfer—enough to send me on a wild goose chase after criminals so good they've never left behind enough evidence or witnesses to implicate them.

All five are behind a laundry list of crimes, but we've never been able to make any charges stick. I have a 'hit list' of five subjects countrywide, and Alan Chase is first on it.

At least he's only a thief. Never violent—just skilled, sneaky. There are men that are guilty of far worse than car theft—especially number five.

But I don't want to think about him. Focus on our Road Runner here.

Alan Chase is an impeccable thief. Not to mention a world-class driver. He could give NASCAR racers a run for their money, according to the one Long Island cop who tried to chase him on the interstate.

"...I never even got close to his bumper. The guy swam through the traffic and the wind and the rain like a damn fish up a stream. He just knew where the holes in the flow of traffic would open up."

"...He didn't endanger anyone, either. Caused a few fender-benders by startling people, but he never knocked into anyone to block my way, didn't drive wrong-way through any areas, never touched the shoulder."

"...He was just gone. I wasn't even able to follow enough to catch it all on dash cam, let alone get a look at his face."

I get up to do a few floor poses for my back and mix up a batch of instant coffee. The old brick hotel has radiators that clank and tick constantly and an elevator that rattles; it sounded like it was going to expire when I brought up my baggage. But it's a lot cozier than the drafty apartment I share with two roommates in Brooklyn.

Guess I'm spending my New Year's working again. But that's all right. No family to go home to anyway.

Alan Chase has been living in Lloyd for three months according to his latest landlord. He likely is involved in the uptick in auto thefts. So I'm stuck here spying on him until we catch him at something or he moves on.

I bring up Chase's photo gallery and frown at his smiling face on my screen. Cute.

Roguish grin, kind of scruffy. Dark auburn hair, dark brows, light brown eyes with a touch of red to them—like sunlight through glasses of sherry. Lean-jawed, athletic, but raw-looking. The kind of guy that lives in jeans.

Hot, but not my type. One of the five I'm chasing is, but I'm trying not to think about him.

If I'm vigilant, smart, and lucky, I'll catch my Road Runner in Lloyd. Otherwise, he'll duck back over the Canadian border to hide, and my boss Daniels will shuffle me off after the next guy after a round of demeaning lectures.

Derek Daniels is a bullying prick with no use for women who won't sleep with him. He sent me out here to confirm that I don't have what it takes to be in the FBI.

I've come here to show he is wrong.

I'm in place. I have contacts, cash for bribes, leads, and a profile. Now, I just have to wait for Chase to make a mistake. Preferably a big one.

Chapter 1
Alan

I've got a weakness for Ford LTDs.
It's completely stupid, I know. But when my grandpa retired, he came home with a Ford LTD Crown Royal he had driven for his cover job, and I loved that car. It was huge, powerful, and drove like a dream.
I learned to drive in that blue LTD. Grandpa's father used to run booze over the border from Canada and had taught him how to drive that big boat of a car like a bat out of hell. Behind its wheel, he taught me everything he knew and then left it to me in his will, and I drove it for ten years.
Subsequently, some drunken piece of shit t-boned it—while it was fucking parked. The sound practically knocked me out of bed by itself. Shattering glass, tearing metal—the death cry of a damn good car.
The bastard was going ninety. Totaled both cars and nearly killed himself. Turns out he mistook the LTD for

one belonging to the dude he thought was fucking his girlfriend.

Why would anyone look for love elsewhere with such a model of loving stability like that guy waiting for her at home? Yikes!

That was the one and only time that my real name ended up on a police report. The law has been after me in several cities, but they never know exactly who they are looking for. I'm a ghost.

A ghost who drives like a demon.

Tonight, I have my sights on a top-of-the-line Ford LTD Crown Victoria, restored from the mid-1980s. Black instead of the dark blue I remember but just as elegant and enormous. Chrome trim, a bench backseat you could fuck in without banging your head on anything. Two big, greasy-looking guys from the city just left her at the far corner of the diner parking lot, and I'm ambling over there now to have a closer look.

The key to going unnoticed late at night is to act casual and relaxed, like you belong. I'm just another guy strolling out of the diner in a hipster watch cap and skinny gray jacket, my hair tucked up out of sight and black-framed glasses covering my eyes.

I picked the outfit at a Goodwill a month ago. I always go incognito when I'm looking for a car to steal. I hadn't planned to take one right out of a parking lot, but for another ride in my favorite kind of car, I'm tempted to risk it. At least nobody will remember details about me that I can't instantly change.

It's a freezing night; my breath steams through the gap in my upturned collar as I cross the parking lot. There's a huge patch of black ice in the middle of the blacktop; I skirt around it nimbly and move on.

Maybe I shouldn't take the car. It's still technically in view of the café windows.

But it's more than nostalgia telling me to take it.

Something in my gut is telling me, too. I notice that the car's lights are on.

Wait...you've got to be kidding me.

The car's rumbling away, exhaust pipe steaming, heater on, and Frank Sinatra playing on a good stereo. The keys are in the damn ignition! It's as if they deliberately left it running so it would keep warm.

This means they're getting a takeout order and will be back in very few minutes. Think fast, Chase!

I go for it!

Without breaking stride, I walk around to the driver's side, open the door with one gloved hand, get in, shut the door, and check around for any surprises. There's a tough purple suitcase shoved onto the back seat. What's in the trunk that they're using passenger space for luggage? I sling my Goodwill backpack next to it. I buckle in and back up smoothly, just like it's my car, and I'm pulling out to drive home.

Nothing to see here, everything's perfectly normal...I drive casual, not too fast, not too slow, keeping away from the patch of black ice.

I make it through the parking lot and maneuver the LTD's front end is into traffic to make the turn, when I hear a shout. In the rearview mirror, I see two fat goons lumbering out in my direction, coats flapping open, gripping white takeout bags and pistols, the glints of chrome warning me.

Oh hell!

One fires and I lurch forward into traffic, hearing the bullet ping off the frozen asphalt. My wheels slip on the icy road before catching a patch of sand and jolting forward. Another bullet follows, whamming off the back bumper.

"Shit! Shit! Shit!"

Cars in the road stop short for me; nobody wants to argue with a giant, old steel-framed car lunging into traffic. I hit the slick road and spin the wheel just enough; the Ford makes the turn—and the light changes at the corner and locks up traffic on every side. Are you kidding me?

Trapped, I turn my worried eyes back to the parking lot. The two argue, one forcing the other one's gun arm down like he doesn't want his car shot up. I can't blame him—especially since I don't want more bullets coming my way.

"Come on," I mutter, counting down the seconds until the light changes. It would be a shitty way to die, holed out over a midrange sedan that hasn't been a hot property since the late nineties.

They notice I'm trapped and start running as fast as they can across the parking lot. Staring at them in horror…I'm sunk! Even if I abandon the car and run across four lanes of traffic, I will be in reach of their bullets. Chase, you're an idiot! This was a really bad idea!

Then a miracle happens! One I probably don't deserve right now. They run out onto that big patch of black ice without noticing it.

The first guy hits it with the heel of his fancy wingtips and does an awkward split, yelling in alarm and accidentally firing into the air. The second guy can't stop in time and crashes into him. They both go down in a heaving tangle. And I finally remember to blink.

Bye, boys! I bark out a laugh as the light changes and the traffic shifts. I ease onto the accelerator as space opens up...and suddenly, I'm free!

The road is my home. Four wheels on the blacktop, enough room to maneuver, and a good car. That's my idea of comfort. And even after years without one, being in a LTD really feels like I belong.

I drive all the way out of Lloyd, not chancing a stop within city limits. I have no idea who those guys were or why they had guns, but it was pretty damn clear they were guarding either the car or something in it.

The suitcase? Or maybe whatever is filling up the trunk? The contents are probably valuable.

I could use a good score before winter really sets in. It started late this year, aside from one big blizzard in mid-November. A little extra capital would be nice before I shut down until next year.

I'm twenty miles Upstate when the LTD's gas meter starts edging toward empty. The nearest town, West Camp, is a few miles off yet: a collection of houses around a church, a few shops, and a gas station connected to an all-night café.

I'll unfortunately need to ditch this vehicle knowing that livid armed men are looking for it. Best to dump it at the edge of town and use another way back to Lloyd.

After I find whatever those guys were guarding, anyway.

I park the LTD in a lot near the end of town. It's late enough that nobody's around except for the café and gas station, blazing with an inviting light. That's good; I need coffee and a warm place to wait for my ride.

First things first, though.

I check the suitcase. It smells of some delicate, expensive perfume, and I find a travel bottle—which is of blue-enameled gold in the shape of a fucking peacock. This suitcase belongs to a wealthy young woman who is either really hot or thinks she is.

There's a half dozen posh, sexy outfits: silk, mostly in shades of blue, including some lingerie for a curvy, busty woman. Not much jewelry, but what's in there would pay rent on my apartment for a few months. A heavy, lined wool winter coat and a pair of surprisingly sensible leather knee boots take up the entire other side.

"Wow. Who did you fuckers steal this from?" I mutter, checking my peripherals before turning back to the case. My fingers trace the fabric lining, encountering several rectangular lumps.

Those are bundles of cash, I'm sure. The smaller lumps feel like more jewelry. Smuggling? Or someone's personal stash?

Good news for me, either way. Finders keepers!

I close the back door and go around to pop the trunk. If they left a jackpot like that in plain view, how valuable is what they hid back here?

This could end up being one hell of a payoff! Maybe even worth almost getting killed for?

I walk back and pull the trunk lid open; the tiny light pops on. I stand there blinking for a moment, staring down.

A large, canvas laundry bag, the heavy kind you can drag four loads in, fills almost the whole space. The curled shape inside sets off alarm bells in the back of my head—especially since instead of the smell of dirty laundry, the delicate scent of that same perfume wafts at me.

"Oh shit!"

I start untying the heavy rope fastening the bag like a giant drawstring and tug the bag opening to loosen it. Almost at once, something makes my heart sink even further: a soft tuft of strawberry blonde hair.

"Please don't be a cadaver." I undo the bag further and tug it down over her face. "Please be alive. I didn't even know you were back here..."

She's beautiful. Soft features go with the lustrous hair and full lips. She's maybe twenty? Her cheeks have color. She breathes.

"Oh, holy crap! Okay. You really scared me for a minute there, lady." I free her from the bag; she's dressed in leather pants and jacket with a silk blouse underneath. She stirs. I notice a small bruise on the side of her neck centered around on a red mark. An injection site?

No wonder she was so still and quiet. She's drugged! Maybe just coming out of it with the cold air hitting her?
"Hey," I pat the side of her sweet face. "Hey, wake up, we've got to move."
Kidnapping? They were kidnapping her! Holy shit, I just rescued a loaded kidnapping victim!
That's promising. Maybe not as promising as walking off with her stuff, but a guy like me always needs more rich friends. Especially if they are heart-breakingly beautiful and owe me big time.
I take her by her shoulders and shake her gently. She stirs, frowning in her sleep, and lets out a soft sigh.
"That's better. Come on back now. I know you're sleepy." I'm starting to worry. The sooner we get out of here, the better; this car might have a LoJack on it…
They may be on their way right now to get their damn car back. And kill me, of course.
I leave her to awaken as I grab my backpack and quickly change my outer clothes. I shake my hair loose and replace it with a fleece-lined deerstalker like a lot of the locals wear. The terribly tight jacket gets replaced by a heavy red plaid coat.
When I get back to her, she's fallen back asleep again.
"Dammit, sweetie, this is not good," I grumble, scooping her out of the trunk and setting her rounded butt on its edge.
She sags forward; I hold her up by the shoulders. Her eyelids flutter—and then fly open.
She stares at me in shock and confusion. She looks quickly around, her sky-blue eyes enormous.

"What—?!?" she gasps, her faint Brooklyn accent sharpening the word.

"Shh, please, don't scream, its okay." What can I say to calm her down? "You're being rescued."

Her mouth closes and she blinks, shaking her head to clear it. "Who are you?"

"Uh, that's a long story. I'll tell you the whole thing once we get out of here."

Chapter 2
Melissa

"Look, it seems you don't like the guy, Melissa, but your dad is not giving you a choice in this. Sorry. I got to do what I'm told, same as you."
That's Benny—big and friendly, always practical. He's the nicer of the two my dad sent after me. The other is Dave: quiet, cold, thoughtful. Scary.
"Enzo tried to rape me, Benny. He wouldn't even wait until we married! He's got two other brothers! If Dad wants me with the Castellos, why not one of them?" I look between them, pleading my case as quietly as my panic will let me.
How did they find me? I was so damn careful! I took the bus, I used cash for everything, I dressed in things I would never wear, all this leather...I look like a biker's whore—and for what?

They found me not even two hours out of the city, and now they're going to drag me home. Drugged. Whatever they shot me up with is already kicking in.

"It's not my call, but I will mention this to your father. Still, you know how he is. Enzo Castello's going to be your future husband. He'll probably be a lot nicer once you're married. He's just enthusiastic because you're hot." His calm, friendly tone never wavers. The other one's staring at me, aware but uncaring, like a cat.

"Please don't," I beg one last time. But it's too late. Benny has brought a laundry cart with an empty bag inside, and I can't move.

I'm sobbing in terror as they put me in the bag.

When I open my eyes again, I think I'm dreaming. A stranger is propping me up on the edge of a car trunk in the cold air. We're somewhere Upstate; it's dark, with the smell of pine trees and snow on the wind.

The man's not Italian. He's hot: tall, dark-haired, and a little scruffy; he has light eyes. I can't place the color of them in the dimness. He's smiling with relief as I try to get my focus back.

"What's your name?" he asks.

"Melissa," I mumble, not giving my last name. Everybody knows it. "You?"

"You can call me Chase." He looks me over, gaze lingering on my face. "Look, I don't know who those guys were that kidnapped you, but we need to get your stuff and ditch this car. Can you walk?"

I hesitate. My legs almost feel steady enough now that the cold is slapping me awake, but I have no idea who this guy is. "I think so. But we need to get all my stuff out of the car before we ditch it, or they'll know where I'm running to."

My stuff and something of Benny's that he always keeps in the glove compartment.

"Grab the suitcase?" I ask. In case he has a gun, I want to keep his hands busy.

"Sure, I'll wrangle it for you. Do you have someone you can call?" His tone is so innocent that I have to choke back my bitter laugh.

"No," I sigh as I get up, leaning heavily on the car, and make my way around to the passenger side. "Nobody close, anyway."

Marcel and Amelie are waiting for me in Montreal. They offered me a place to stay when I made a run for the Canadian border. They have no idea that I picked Montreal because Dad is terrified of the crime family that controls the city; the less they know about my problems, the safer we'll all be.

I have to make sure that my father never knows the names of the friends that are helping me. My phone is full of our conversations and Benny took it. He stashed it in the glove compartment.

"I have to get my phone. Then we can go. Do you have a way out of town?"

"I'm working on that. We can wait at the café until my ride back to Lloyd gets here." I hear his soft grunt as he pulls my suitcase out of the back. He's so friendly and cheerful...but not like Benny. He sounds baffled, like he's still getting used to the idea that he found a woman in the trunk.

So either he's a very good actor, or he's genuinely shocked to have found me.

I pull the side door open and unlatch the glove compartment. My phone slides off a pile of old folded maps and spills into my hand. Then the holstered .38 revolver tucked behind it slides out, too.

I catch it. It's heavy in my hand. It's been a season since I fired one, but I'm not planning to do so now.

I just need answers.

He comes around with the suitcase in his hands and the start of a sentence on his lips, and then he just blinks at me holding the gun. I don't hold it on him directly, but I don't hold it away from him either.

"I'm sorry, but I just got drugged and stuffed in a trunk by mobsters, and I'm not in a trusting mood. How do you fit into all of this?"

Chase is blinking at me in shock, like I totally destroyed my own image. This clearly isn't a violent guy.

"Come on, don't make me point this at you. I actually hate guns," I sigh.

"Me, too. Uh, well, the simple answer is, I stole the car." He smiles awkwardly as he keeps his hands in view—which makes him look even cuter.

"What?" I lower the gun slightly, and he relaxes. This guy isn't used to having guns held on him. "You stole...Benny's car?"

"Yeah, okay?" He winces. "I stole the car, got out of Lloyd, and then realized you were in the back and set you free. Who the hell is Benny?"

I'm not ready to get into that atrocious story yet. I'm an inch from crying. "I'll ask the questions. Do you have a secure place in Lloyd?"

"Uh...yeah, my house..." He looks at me worriedly. "What are you planning?"

"I need to shake these guys off. You just stole from them, so you need to shake them off, too." I think about it a moment longer, then holster the gun and tuck it into the back of my leather pants. "Is hiding out in Lloyd part of your plan?"

"Until things cool off, yeah." He looks increasingly worried, despite my putting the gun away. "Look, I don't mean to pry into your business, but uh...what kind of trouble are you running from here?"

I look at Chase for a few moments, and then sigh. "Not here. Let's...go someplace warm and wait for your ride."

The café is a 1950s revival burger shop. I change into my wool coat before heading there, and cover my hair with his watch cap. My new friend suggested the change of clothes.

He's done this car theft thing before. A lot.

He pulls out a cheap smartphone and starts texting as we walk down the windswept street toward the open café.

"You never told me what I'm rescuing you from," Chase reminds me. "Or why you want to hide out at my place."

"Look, I'll give you the short form now. My dad's a monster; he wants me to marry another monster. Those two guys you ditched work for him." My lips start trembling and I press them together. I really don't want to cry around this guy.

"Monster—or mobster?" he asks quietly.

Tears spring to my eyes, and I take a sad, shivery breath. "Both," I mumble.

"Okay, okay. You're still drugged, you don't know me, let's get you collected, and warmed up."

He touches my shoulder and I suppress another surge of tears.

"I didn't expect anybody to step in, even by accident," I admit. "I'm still stunned."

"Uh, yeah, that's logical. I'm still surprised to find you." That awkward laugh. Boyish, but gentle.

I like him. And not just because he saved my ass. Or because he's actually really hot.

"What's your plan for getting us out of here?" I ask urgently. "Dad's men probably won't expect you to double back to Lloyd."

"Yeah, they never do." He scratches his chin. "A wrecker is coming for the car and another coming for us. ETA half an hour."

"A wrecker? Tell your guy to look for a LoJack." I worry, and he nods texting for another moment.

"It's all right, the guy's a pro, and he'll deal with it." He tucks the phone back in his pocket. "You uh...really need to hide out somewhere?"

The look I give him is probably pretty desperate. "Just for the night. I can't get to the other place right now." Gun or no gun, I'm working on trusting him.

If he's a nonviolent thief, one thing will convince him: the cash I'm stashing. "I can pay you."

"Uh..." His gaze flicks over me and that awkward smile returns. "Okay then...Melissa. A thousand bucks a night; you follow my instructions, and tell me the full story of what's going on."

He'd probably suggest something else, too, but he's gentleman enough not to bring it.

That says good things about him by itself. How will he react to the whole story? Maybe he'll even be outraged, like Marcel was when I told him what Enzo did?

That would be a nice change of pace. "Done. So what's the plan?" Now that I'm away from my father's goons, I have a few options for traveling anonymously to the border. But another idea is forming in my head.

How nice is this guy? How good a driver? And how interested is he in money?

"We sit tight for a while, things cool down, you move on." He sighs. "And I retire for the season."

"You mean from stealing cars?"

"That and some courier work—anything involving driving a lot. It's not all that workable in the snow, so I take winters off."

I'm thinking fast as we reach the café. "Can I interest you in one more delivery job before you shut down for the year?"

We go quiet until we're seated and the chubby waitress has taken our coffee orders and sailed off. "What did you have in mind?" he asks.

I look up at him—and pause, taken aback by the color of his eyes now that we're in good light. They're golden brown with a faint copper overtones, quite jewel-like. "I need to make a delivery to Montreal within the next few days." I can get a message to my friends and let them know I'm running late.

"What's the package?" he asks as he examines the menu. I don't even look at mine. I'm too queasy from the drug hangover to eat.

I put on the bravest smile. "Me."

Chapter 3
Alan

So she wants a lift to Montreal? It's not my first border run. The last guy was running from the cops, not the mob. Less rules—more danger.
As I'm mulling this over, the burner phone buzzes.
I check the screen. Marty is messaging me back. I'm here. Check for the LJ first, it'll be high end. If this is a mobster's car, it may have more nasty surprises than just a tracking device. And that's bad enough.
I look back up at Melissa. "I can do that, but let's talk over the specifics and lay some ground rules. This will cost you." I keep my eyes on her face. My gaze keeps trying to graze the front of her coat, like I'm hoping to see through the layers of wool and leather.
My judgment is weird right now. It's not every damn night you get to rescue a drugged, kidnapped, and very hot woman who is running from the mob. From her father the mob boss, I should say.

Oh yeah, honey, if I'm sheltering you from your dad and taking you across the border, you're going to pay a lot more than a thousand a night.

But only in cash. She smoking hot, and the shy way she looks at me piques my interest. Even if I'm risking my neck for her, some things are given, never earned.

That's not going to stop me from getting as much as possible in the cash department, though. Call it hazard pay.

My phone beeps again. Found it. It's got some extra wiring. Should I deactivate?

I stiffened slightly. No. Is it on the inside of the bumper?

Yes, the back one. Why?

Don't mess with the extra wires. Don't deactivate. Just remove the whole back bumper and leave it right there.

"What's wrong?" she asks me softly as she perches her chin on the backs of her wrists. Cute, but not flirtatious. Her eyes are dull with exhaustion.

"You were right about the LoJack. He's leaving it behind without deactivating it. He found some other wires."

"You told him not to mess with them?" Her voice lowers uncomfortably.

"Yeah. Don't worry; he doesn't have his head up his ass." Stealing vehicles for a living, you need ways of unloading them without leaving a trail behind. I leave city limits, hand the keys to a transport guy disguised as a car wrecker, and have him tow it after paying me my advance. The rest of my cut comes afterwards.

Our coffee comes, and I order us both a slice of apple pie.

"Just try it," I ask her gently, more than troubled about her drug hangover.

"Okay," she murmurs.

I check my phone. No more complications, comes the message. You'll only get $1k on this.

Send it after, I reply. Thanks for coming out in the cold. See you in the spring.

No problem, brother. Happy New Year.

"Okay, the tow's handled," I said quietly and grabbed my coffee. I was pretty glad I wouldn't be driving on the way back. "Our ride should be here in about ten minutes. We'll meet him outside."

The pie's pretty good, tasting more of actual apples and spices than sugar. Melissa nibbles on hers doggedly, her eyes enormous and vulnerable despite the gun in the back of her pants. I know she hung onto it because she doesn't know me, and I don't blame her, but when she pulled it on me, it put a hell of a chill down my spine.

I don't do guns. I know gun safety, how to aim, fire, and fix one. But I hate them. I have actually seen what they can do, and I don't mess with them. The only thing not freaking me out about the fact that she pulled one on me is that she seemed eager to put it away.

"I still can't believe this is happening," she mumbles. She's holding back tears again. I've watched her fight them off since she opened her eyes.

"You mean that you escaped?" I drain the last of my mug and set it down at the edge of the table.

She nods. "Um...yeah, I almost gave up. I should thank you."

"Well," I lean forward to look her in the eyes. "You're welcome. I sure as fuck hope someone else would do the same for me."

Why do I give so much of a damn about this girl? She's paying me to look after her—maybe even get her to the border. She's had a shitty time—but I'm a thief, not a saint. Getting tangled up with her—mainly emotionally—will be hazardous.

She sips at her coffee and then sets it down, dumping a lot of sugar and cream into it. "Too strong," she murmurs.

"Assume that your freedom's permanent." The more I think about it, the more it pisses me off. Who does this crap to their own daughter? "Fear will drain you, and believe me, if you want a ride, you're hiring the best. Going to cost you, though."

"I can pay whatever you ask," she says with quiet confidence. "I just need to get to my friends."

It would really be nice to start the winter a step closer to prosperous. "What are you thinking?"

The waitress comes by to pour my refill, and Melissa busies herself picking at her pie. With her glorious hair tucked up and her body hidden in the coat, she looks like a child: big-eyed and vulnerable.

She swipes a figure into her phone and slides it across to me.

I take it. My eyes widen. 500k.

Off goes the waitress again, and I blink at her. "There's got to be a story behind why it's that much."

"Yeah. But I'm not spilling the whole thing until we're alone." She tucks her phone back in her purse and looks up at me. "Okay?"

I nod. "Sounds fair." The more I think about this, the more it sounds like hazard pay. Just who the heck is her father?

"Just so you know," I tell Melissa when we walk out of the café. "The driver has no idea what is going on. He's been fed a cover story. We're a married couple going back to Lloyd. You're not feeling well."

"I'm not," she admits quietly. "I wonder what they shot me up with."

"Drink a lot of water and sports drinks to flush your system. I suspect it was a heavy sedative."

"Makes sense. Almost feels like the stuff they give you at the dentist. That always leaves me queasy." Her foot slips on the icy sidewalk, and I grab her arm quickly.

She catches her breath and gets her feet steadied. "Thanks."

"No problem." A burgundy SUV is idling at the corner. "That's us. Let's get you settled."

The driver's got an Uber tag in the corner of his dash, and Melissa gives me a startled look. "Come on, sweetheart," I reassure, getting into character as I move up to greet the driver. "We're almost home."

She's still wary of me. I'm still wary of her. But I'll take a risk for a good cause...especially for half a million dollars.

Chapter 4
Melissa

As soon as we get underway in the warm car, I feel sedated again. Why are my instincts telling me to trust this thief? He claims to be the best driver in New York State. He's my best ticket across the border.
He puts his arm around me as I rest against his shoulder. He smells of mint and coffee and the spices from the pie. He's so gentle...
I don't know anything about gentle men. Benny is maybe the closest to that, and he pretty much fails at it entirely. My father rules by fear, both family and Family. My brothers are his cold-eyed drones. His men aren't much better; not a one of them would ever consider crossing Don Gianni Lucca.
But here's this guy, touching me so lightly, the heat of his hand radiating against my cheek. It's...comforting.
"Did your car break down?" the Uber driver asks Chase. He's a narrow-faced man with dark, scruffy hair. Chase is

using a gift card and a burner phone; he'll get his money without leaving much of a trail.

"Yeah, and my lady's got a migraine." His voice is so kind. Please don't let this be an appalling trick!

"Oh, that's terrible. My lector gets those all the time." He smiles briefly, and to my surprise, he's wearing a white band collar.

A priest is driving us? Oh great, we're lying to a priest! If I wasn't going to hell for being a mob boss's daughter, I sure am now.

Then again, he's getting paid, and we're getting a safe, nondescript ride to Lloyd. We don't exactly owe the guy our life story.

The two men chat quietly as we drive on through the dark. Slowly, I lean my head on Chase's broad shoulder and close my eyes, pulling the hood of my coat over my face against oncoming headlights. Please, actually be this good.

We're on the road for twenty minutes before I hear the rushing sound of several cars headed toward us at once. I lift my head, and watch the headlights coming.

"Goodness," the priest is saying, "That almost looks like a funeral procession."

My heart rate picks up. Without lowering my hood, I see three big black sedans driving by. Matching sedans— from my father's motor pool.

Oh my God, Benny and Dave brought backup to Lloyd. Please don't let this be the only car they pass before they get to town!

I turn my face away and bury it in Chase's shoulder as he covers the back of my hood with his hand, still in character. "Shh, sweetie, those lights are pretty bright. Just keep your eyes closed."

But I can't relax, even with his touch and his low, reassuring voice. Tears squirt through my eyelashes and I mash my face against the flannel of his sleeve until the sound of their engines fades off in the distance.

Only then do I lift my head and meet Chase's worried gaze. He nods, understanding my unexpected attack of fear. "It's okay," he reassures.

I let out my breath and straighten, but I'm so tired that soon I settle against him again.

"Won't be long now," the priest reassures in a cheerful voice.

I close my eyes in relief and drift off.

I don't remember when we pull up at the narrow Victorian house with its brown patch of a front yard and windows blocked by blackout drapes. I just remember being removed from the car. My suitcase wheels rattle against the slate sidewalk as Chase helps me inside while pulling it.

The house is warm, a few lights are on giving the small wood-floor living room a golden glow. A small Christmas tree is set up with a bunch of model cars circling it by the wet bar, and there is a gas fireplace he turns on as soon as he gets me out of the coat and on the couch.

"We got away clean," he reassures me when he sees my expression. He takes off that goofy redneck cap and the matching jacket and stuffs them into his backpack before throwing it into a closet. Underneath, he's wearing a clingy green turtleneck of some high-tech material.

I hesitate in answering, my eyes caught by the curves of his muscular back as they show through his shirt.

...Oh.

He's a lot fitter than I expected. Lean, but powerful, with the easy grace of a dancer. When he looks back at me and smiles, his eyes twinkling, my breath catches in my throat.

"So," he says, lifting an eyebrow slightly at the sight of me staring. "You want to tell me who your father is, for starters?"

I nod and struggle to focus for a few moments before looking back into those beautiful eyes. "Don Gianni Lucca."

His eyes widen, and he sits back, suddenly looking plenty worried. "...Shit."

"Yeah." My smile is an apologetic half-wince. "That's why I'm offering you the big money."

He seems to consider this for a moment, and then nods. "Okay. So...tell me how you ended up on the run from the most dangerous mobster on the East Coast?"

He's apprehensive. Is he going to dump me as a client? He needs to understand how desperate this is!

It will matter to him. He's a nice guy.

I hope.

"My father had three sons and one daughter. He wanted four sons. My mother is deceased."

Chase is sitting in one of the big, brown leather chairs across from the matching couch I'm lounging on. Since I sat down, his glance has slid up my leg every now and then, but the moment I speak, they're back on my face. I go on.

"All the old mobsters who come by and eat our food and drink our booze and pinch my ass won't let their daughters near him no matter how many gifts he offers. Most of them don't care much for their daughters, but they care enough not to let them end up smuggled out the door in a rolled up carpet like my mom did." He's sitting there listening, his brows drawing together, golden-brown eyes full of quiet revulsion.

I pause. Dammit, what a nice guy. I really shouldn't be dragging him into my problems, but he's my best hope. "I'm sorry. This is all appalling, but...you wanted the truth."

He presses his lips together and looks down at his hands. "You know, I'd be making you a hot toddy right now, but I'm thinking booze probably won't mix well with that sedative." Then he looked up at me. "How did you know about...what happened to your mom?"

"My brother Joey told me when he was drunk and home from the Army. I was ten. I've been terrified of my father ever since." I don't know why, but instead of the usual fear, what I feel now is...poignant. I would have liked to have known Mom.

"There are a lot of arranged weddings in the mob. It was for my Mom, too. Her dad was an industrialist with a pile of cash that went straight into Dad's pocket. Now my Dad wants to marry me off to a son of the Don of Chicago. A guy named Enzo."

My lips feel very dry, like they're about to crack. I fish nervously for the little globe of strawberry cream lip balm in my bag and rub it on my mouth, but it doesn't help much.

He gets up and brings me a dark blue sports drink that smells faintly of raspberry when I crack it open. "Go on." I take a sip—and then find myself swallowing down half of it in several large gulps. "Oh God." Some of my headache goes away almost at once. "Thank you."

I have to take a moment. "Enzo's...dreadful." I take the watch cap off and shake my hair out before handing him the hat. "His dad got tired of paying off girlfriends' hospital bills and decided to marry him off."

"To you." He opens his own sports drink, staring at me with a frown.

"Yeah. But he decided—" My voice gets shaky and I take another swallow, trying to steady it. "He wanted a piece of me early. That's uh...that's why I ran."

I don't have to elaborate. He already sympathizes. I can see it in his face, his body language. It's pronounced and genuine. His jaw is dropped. He's revolted.

He blanches in aversion. "Jesus. You okay?"

"Yeah, he um...I kind of..." I swallow hard, the fear of that moment ghosting through and fading away again. "He tried it, and he's bigger than me, but uh...I get mean when I panic, and he kind of found out the hard way."

He blinks slowly, some of the dismay draining from his face. "Wait. What?"

"He got a...thousand dollar bottle of Chianti to the side of his head." How fast some mild embarrassment can displace that ghostly fear? Between this and the gun, he might think I'm cruel.

"Wait, you knocked him out?"

I think back to that moment, pinned on a pool table in Enzo's den, his drunken rage... Barely reaching the stem of the bottle and then gripping it hard as he shoved his pants down.

His greasy boner was the size of my thumb and went limp when I clocked him. I shoved him off me to the floor, grabbed the unbroken bottle, uncorked it, and when he started waking up, I just started feeding him wine until he passed out again for good. He never fully opened his eyes.

Didn't actually protest much either, now that I think about it.

"Yeah, basically. Then I went upstairs, cleaned out Dad's safe and left."

Chase's handsome face splits in a wide, lopsided grin. "Holy shit, you're a badass! What the hell do you need me for?"

I'm taken aback. "I...uh...well, remember, when I tried to get to Montreal on my own, I was caught within two hours."

They were waiting for me in a hotel room. I cried and pleaded, but of course, they weren't about to let me go. You can't expect mercy from mob guys. I've grown up knowing that.

His smile fades. "Oh. Yeah. Sorry, you probably didn't need the cue."

I give him a tiny smile to bolster his. "It's okay.

"So, that's in essence the story," I say quietly. "If I don't get to my friends in Canada, my dad will force me to marry Enzo. Probably after letting Enzo...punish me."

He sets his jaw and his feral-looking eyes flash. "Nah, they'll never have the chance, Princess. Come through with the cash, and you'll get your ride out to Montreal. I have a pretty good advantage."

And then comes that lopsided grin again, dazzling and distracting me from my fear of Dad.

My mouth is dry again. I take a drink and hope he doesn't notice me staring. "What's that?"

He winks. "I've never been caught."

Chapter 5
Alan

"Enzo won't marry me if I'm not a virgin, Chase," Melissa is purring in my ear. I feel her warm, full breasts slide against my chest in the dark as my dick comes to attention. "You've done so much for me. Do you mind doing...this one last thing?"
"At your service, Princess," I gasp hoarsely, not sure where my clothes have gone and not giving a shit.
We kiss, and her mouth tastes like wine. Her voice lowers to whimpers as I run my lips down her neck. I cup the globes of her ass and feel my cock rise to brush against the downy delta of her thighs. I lay her down to thrust into her and my eyes open wide in pain as the jeans I fell asleep in flatten a boner the size of Florida.
Reaching for my groin, I roll over, grunting in discomfort—and I forget that I slept on the couch. I fall

off and knock my forehead against the plank floor.
"Aah—fuck. Ow. Why?"
I finally manage to unzip the fly and ease the chafing pressure of the denim on my dick, which is blue-steel hard and probably wondering where the lustful naked chick went. Then I roll over with a sigh, the center of my forehead stinging. "Well that was fun," I mutter.
I just had to be a gentleman and give Melissa my bed. No chance of joining her. I'm a stranger, even if we felt a spark between us. Besides, she's exhausted, recovering from the drugs, and fearful.
So, the couch for me. It was long enough but apparently...not wide enough. And that dream...
Guess I like her more than I want to admit. But that's yet another reason to be considerate.
I unzip my fly completely to sit up. Damn, do I need a cold shower? That's going to be awkward if my guest gets up for a drink of water.
I get up and turn to face the living room window. The house backs onto a drop-off; across the gap, there's a three-story brick parking structure. Fortunately it's deserted now—
A faint sound of something falling onto concrete makes me look up. My eyes adjust to the dim streetlights, and I realize someone is standing on the rim of the parking structure, bent over the edge and reaching futilely after whatever fell down. Someone in a long, dark overcoat—and with long, pale hair.

Woops, woops, just showed a random chick my crank, yay. Just the thing to make myself look like Lloyd's resident perv. I hurriedly draw the curtains. "Crap."

The house is small, narrow, and weird, renting cheap because of it despite being a stand-alone. There's the undersized living room, a kitchen, and a big room I've turned into my home gym on the ground floor, with a bathroom, a bedroom, and my office on the second. There's barely any outside space, but I don't care; I'll be moving on from Lloyd at the end of winter anyway.

I walk up the stairs for my cold shower, wondering where I should go after Montreal. It'll be a lonely New Year's, unless of course Melissa feels like doing something up in Canada. Might be nice, despite the cold—I bet she'll warm up to me plenty when she's no longer running for her life.

I kind of hope she calms down enough to ditch the gun eventually if we're going to date, though. It feels eerie having it in the house.

Most guys in the business think I'm crazy for not having a gun. They assume I'm a pacifist—and I am, to some degree, but not because I won't meet force with force. A gun is an ultimate solution to an often temporary problem.

I have enough skills in other areas to control the amount of force to use in a situation—often even when dealing with someone else with a gun. You can't shoot someone a little bit. But there's a big spectrum of options between subduing someone, kicking their ass, and killing them if your body is your weapon.

I also have some pretty personal reasons for not liking guns. Call it the Batman Motive. There's a big reason I was raised by my grandpa instead of my dad. And just like Bruce, I saw the whole thing.

Melissa has a pistol she's using as a last resort. It's in her bag now. I'm wary of it—but I'm not wary of her.

More like I'm worried about her. On top of wanting her. My dick is still hard as I scrub off. I consider taking care of it, but I get distracted by my thoughts. I am about to help a Mafia princess get away from her demon father. That is dangerous, even for a witty guy like me. But then again, these guys are already pissed off at me. I stumbled into this situation and got on their bad side by mistake.

I figure that I should take the risk of helping Melissa. And not just because I want to fuck her.

I'm not the kind of guy who gets stuck on women often. I love them; they're wonderful and not just to fuck. But I haven't been serious with anyone yet.

I've never had a bad breakup. Just a string of lovers turned friends, who still sometimes come back for a booty call when they're between relationships, or when their men won't get them off.

From Melissa's story, she's a virgin. My dream made it absurdly clear how much the idea of being her first turns me on. I would totally love to spoil her so she comes back for more. Or maybe...never wants anyone else? Wait, where did that come from? Come on man, that's your dick doing the thinking. You're getting a half a million bucks to take her safely to Montreal. That's good enough.

Once I'm done with the shower, my slowly relaxing cock gets in a pair of green boxers, and I stroll quietly into the bedroom, drying off my hair with a towel. I cross to the closet to pull on fresh clothes, looking back now and again at my guest.

In the light from the bathroom, I can see Melissa curled on my bed under a mound of comforters. I smile, remembering her complaining of a chill and me just pulling more out of the linen closet and piling them on until she started giggling.

I'm a romantic. Not a very traditional one, but I've got my ideals, and my feelings on how women should be treated. When I found out she was going to be sold off to a guy who tried to violate her, I had to do something. Now, though, things are getting beyond business or idealism—and more personal.

Okay, so I'm attracted, sympathetic, and I like her. I still don't actually know her well.

She lets out a soft whimper. I take a few steps toward her as I catch the gleam of a tear on her cheek. I don't even wonder what she's dreaming about.

I pull my shirt on, and then put decorum aside and reach down to gently shake her shoulder. She gasps awake with an alarmed look and sits up—and then her fingers claw into the front of my shirt and she starts crying.

I go rigid...and then slide my arms around her, burying my nose in her soft cloud of copper hair for a moment before lowering my lips to her ear.

"Melissa? Melissa—it's all right, it was a nightmare. You're safe!" I murmur, holding her close.

"Don't let go," she mumbles against my chest, and my arms tighten around her. She's trembling, her heart beating so fast it distracts me from the soft push of her breasts against me.

Most of me, anyway. My cock's already waking up as I breathe in her soft vanilla and rose scent. I hope she doesn't notice.

I run my hand down the back of her hair and feel her relax against me, her sobs and sniffles drying up. "It's okay," I reassure. "You're with me. You're still free. Everything will be all right."

It takes her a few minutes to pull herself together as I sit on the edge of the bed and cuddle her, and the whole time, she doesn't pull away from me. I hold her, my eyes closed, trying to ignore how my own heart is pounding, or how images from the dream leave me shaking with restrained desire.

I could make you feel so good right now, I think feverishly as I comfort her. *I could make all of this go away.*

But I won't even propose it. I'm not that guy, no matter how much my cock aches for her. You don't have success with women by treating them like meat.

Finally, she lifts her face from my chest and looks up at me. Her eyes are full of humiliation. "Thank you. I've got to look a mess right now."

"You're beautiful," I say softly and mean it.

She stops short and blinks at me, a flicker of longing in her eyes again. It leaves me shuddering with desire. *Can't we just...?*

"You're having a really rough night. Don't fret about not being camera ready. I really don't give a shit." I reach down and tuck strands of her hair behind her ear, and she swallows, gazing at me almost worshipfully for a moment.

Those eyes. Wide, blue, full of timid invitation, her gaze affecting me like hands caressing my body. I swallow, knowing at once what's going to happen if I stay.

"Thank you," she finally manages, and I feel the soft warmth of her small hand on the back of mine. "For everything."

"Just pay me and promise you'll work with me getting you to Montreal. You'll be with your friends just after New Year's." My voice is hoarse.

"Yes. I'll do all of that." Her hand. Those eyes. She wants me to stay here and join her.

But if I do, she may not be ready for what happens next.

"I should...go back downstairs," I breathe, and she frowns.

"Why?"

"Because I don't think I could stop at just holding you." I gently back away from her, caressing my hand down her back one last time. "I'm sorry."

"Don't be." She gives me a sad smile as she withdraws. "You're the first guy to want me and actually hold off." That makes me feel good, even while I ache with sexual frustration. "We'll pick this conversation back up later." And I wink and force myself to leave.

Chapter 6
Melissa

For the first time since escaping my father's men, I'm not thinking about that terrible situation. I'm too preoccupied with waking up to a caring embrace and how Chase and I almost kissed. That was so pleasant. I'm not used to that. I'm not used to a man's touch feeling good.

My time in Chase's arms has affected me peculiarly. I'm at peace, but I can't fall asleep. My spirits are up, but I can't fully relax. My skin feels so sensitized that the soft sheet caresses me where my nightgown doesn't cover. And when the silk of the gown brushes against my skin, a tingle rushes through me. It leaves me craving more—more of his touch, more of his warmth, more of that tenderness.

I really wish he stayed. But I wouldn't know what to do if he had. Feeling something besides dread or disgust for a

man is so strange. That first taste of real desire made me want to lunge after it...but I'm not ready.
Is it because he rescued me? Is he my 'type'? Is it him in particular? Or is it because he's the first guy who's actually done right by me?
I'm still suspicious. He might want me sexually, but men can fuck even if they hate you. Some of them are nice strictly because they want to fuck.
I saw his eyes trying to trace my body even through my coat. He rescued me and he didn't have to. Maybe that means he cares about me outside of getting what he wants?
Maybe that's what normal people do, and I've been surrounded by horrible shitheads my whole life.
Or, this could all be about sex and money. That thought gives me a strange relief. It may have nothing to do with the idea of kindness or caring? Simplifying his motives down to my payment and his yearning is easier to wrap my head around.
Except...if it really was that simple, would he have been gallant like that and left? Maybe I turned him off somehow. That hurts to think about.
As I lie there, soft sounds come from downstairs. The door to the bedroom is right by the stairway, which bottoms out next to his living room. A soft curse. Grunts. Panting.
Quietly, I get up and tip toe across the room. I make it to the doorway and see the top of Chase's head as he sits on the couch.

He curses softly through his teeth and pants harder. I lean forward to look—and lean back instantly, blushing. Oh.

That glimpse of him pumping that enormous, very stiff cock in one fist proves it. He's horny and didn't want to push anything. He's...doing precisely what he said.

Wow. He's extremely honest for a thief. Or for a guy for that matter.

...Which leads me back to wishing he stayed. Oh well. It's not like we won't be spending time together over the next few days. There will be plenty of chances.

I'm about to return to bed when I notice something unusual. A light—a circular light, weaving back and forth against the shade covering the living room window. I blink at it for a moment, and then quickly realize it's a beam from a flashlight.

Chase lets out a grunt of dissatisfaction; cloth rustles and he shuffles over to the window; his sweatpants are up but there is an enormous awning in the front. He pries apart two of the blinds to look between them. "The hell?" he mumbles.

A pause. I duck back into the shadows, not wanting him to know I was...watching him. Including getting a good look at the massive tool pushing out the front of his sweats. The sight has half of me wondering how it would fit inside me, while the other half is determined to try.

He suddenly curses under his breath and moves away from the window hastily. "Melissa!"

I back up by the bed before I answer. "Yes?"

"Get dressed as fast as you can and grab your stuff. We've got to go."

A rush of adrenaline spikes through me. I don't ask why—I just grab my leathers and yank them on. I check my purse for the phone and the gun and stomp into my boots. Chase is bustling downstairs.

I scurry down to join him, grabbing the handle of my purple suitcase. "What is it?"

"You know those black sedans that passed us on the highway?"

I go cold inside. "Yes."

"Three just pulled up outside." He zips up his jacket and grabs the suitcase from me, tucking it under his arm. "Let's move."

Oh God. I forget all about asking him who the person with the flashlight was. Maybe he has a lookout? Ask later, run now.

"How the hell did they find us?" I pant as we race through the kitchen toward the back exit.

"I don't know, but we've got to get out of here. Can you climb?" He unlocks the back door and shoves it open, and we plunge into the icy night. Before the back door has even closed behind us, heavy fists pound on the front door.

"I'll manage." My stomach flips over; I've been shut inside and stuffed into pretty dresses with few chances for climbing or any other kind of play. But I'm not about to slow him down now.

Outside, the tiny backyard drops off quickly into a dark ravine. There is water at the bottom; it's maybe thirty feet deep. There's a hole in the old wooden fence; he helps me through and briefly shines his tactical light on a rope ladder.

An ordinary rope hangs next to it. He grabs that and looks at me. "Okay. Do not rush. Just get down as fast as you can. It's slippery, so be careful."

I nod, my heart in my throat, doubly glad for the boots and leather. I tighten my purse against my shoulder. "Okay."

"I'll be waiting for you at the bottom," he says, and jumps backward, rappelling expertly out of sight.

Wow. That was swift. The sound of someone kicking the front door alerts me, and I grab the rope ladder, putting my trembling foot on the first rung and scrambling awkwardly down.

It's terrifying: a sightless climb down a slippery, muddy slope streaked with ice, while icy water drips into my hair from above. The rope ladder wobbles; my legs shake from fear as I hunt around for the next rung with my foot.

I'm scared. I'm going to fall. Or they'll catch me on this damn ladder, unable to go any further.

"Hey, are you all right?" Chase calls up softly. "I can't see you."

"I'm going as fast as I can," I stammer apologetically, forcing myself down another two rungs. My foot slips, and I almost lose my footing on the next rung; I grab the ropes and freeze, panting in panic.

Suddenly, the ladder shakes slightly, and I hear a soft thump. Chase is climbing up the rope beside me. "Hey. It's all right."

My shivering stops, and my death grip on the ropes loosens enough for me to feel my fingertips again. "I'm sorry,"

"Shh, don't worry about it. Come down the ladder one step at a time. I'll grab you if you slip. I promise." His voice is so kind, even with the solid urgency behind it.

I come close to slipping once more. He hears my gasp and firmly grabs the back of my leather jacket. Just his touch is enough to steady me some, and I pull myself together and continue.

At last, my feet hit the muddy bed of a temporary stream. Icy water tugs against my ankles; I bless the boots once more for keeping my feet dry, but my toes are getting cold fast. My eyes have adjusted; in the thin light trickling through the pine boughs, Chase turns around and grabs the ladder and the rope.

"Give me a second." He gives them both a hard yank and twist, and then pulls them sideways with a grunt of effort. I hear two pings as their mountings pop free, and they slither down the slope. He throws the bundle under a tree, and then grabs my hand in one and my suitcase in the other.

"Okay," he uttered. "Let's go. Follow me, and try not to slip."

We hasten through the four-inch torrent. Mud sucks at the bottoms of my boots; rocks and branches trip me, but not enough to cause more than a stumble. I struggle, drawing strength from the grip of his hand.

Someone is yelling behind us; they probably discovered the back door was unlocked. Shouts and swearing echo from the top of the drop-off. I gasp, lungs burning, and run even faster. Please don't let them see us.

"There's a culvert up ahead," he urges, and we plunge into it a moment later, just as Benny's voice reaches our ears.

"What do you mean you lost them?" he roars, and then we're running into the dark with only Chase's petite flashlight to light our way.

Chapter 7
Alan

I have to give Melissa credit: she's a trooper. She's not used to dodging; her grunts of exertion make that clear. But I'm really glad she got over it with a little encouragement.

Another rope ladder is set up a hundred yards past the culvert. She climbs first; she's better going up though she whimpers her way.

I end up tying the suitcase to the bottom of the ladder and pulling it up after me. We emerge from behind some evergreen bushes into a small park. "This way," I take her hand again, leading her through an empty playground.

At last we reach the curb, where my escape vehicle is waiting. It's a big, completely nondescript panel truck, the sort you see making deliveries day and night all over the country. Inside, it's full of surprises, but right now, it's the heated cab and powerful engine that will serve us the most.

She stares when I roll up the rear door to toss her suitcase into the back. There's plenty of room in there, almost like a camper van—except heavily insulated and armored. I set the purple case inside and close it up. "Let's get out of here."

The engine rumbles to life on the first try, and the heaters start blowing warm air. Melissa sighs with relief shivering beside me, but she doesn't open her eyes until we've been underway for over a minute.

"You okay?" I ask her, and she nods mutely.

"I'm getting there," she manages several seconds later and surreptitiously wipes her eyes. "Just really glad you know what you're doing."

"Yeah, well, I'm just glad you didn't choke on me. Not really anyway. But I'm still trying to figure out how the hell they found us."

"I have no idea. Did they see your face? My father has some decent computer and tech guys. Benny is one of them—when he's not kidnapping people." She sounds so miserable.

"Maybe. But I don't think so. This place isn't even under my name, and the landlord doesn't have my photo on file."

It's a real concern. Somehow they managed to find us. And if it wasn't for some stranger shining their flashlight on my blinds, I wouldn't have seen that procession of black cars about to make the turn across the culvert onto my street.

"But somehow they found us—and someone gave

us a warning as well. And I have no idea who it was." I think back to the person on top of the parking structure, mulling the possibilities as I drive us down the almost-deserted street.

Right now, as we talk, the fucking mobsters are probably tearing apart my rental house looking for anything personal—anything that can tell them who I am or who my associates are. Joke's on them; anything that's remotely personal is in safe deposit boxes and secure storage units outside of Lloyd. It still feels like a violation, and deep down, it's still pissing me off.

Should Melissa's be the one to be angry with? If she made a mistake, it was probably unintentional. So with a gentle voice, I say, "No to be accusing, but I have to ask you a few questions."

She tenses beside me, but it's not a surprise. Women who have been brutalized by men expect more of the same from other men, especially when things get tense. Fortunately, I'm not some brute who turns on women like that, even if they screw up.

"Did you tell anyone where you were, even by accident?" My voice is calm and my eyes are on the road. "It's okay if you did, but I need to know."

"I told my friends in Montreal there is a delay, but with no specifics." She double checks her phone. "I didn't share my location to anyone, by accident or otherwise."

"Do you have your GPS or Wi-Fi on?" I don't know huge amounts about electronics outside of automotive computer and electrical systems. But basic phone security is pretty straightforward—and yet not widely known enough.

"No, I've been keeping it in airplane mode when I'm not using it because my father keeps calling. I just check for messages from authentic friends occasionally." She gives me a nervous look. "Could they have tracked it?"

"Not likely," That means we still have no damn idea how he tracked her. Electronics, maybe? "Does your dad always seem to know where you are?"

"It's never came up. He never let me go out without an escort." Her voice shakes.

"Oh." Damn. "We found a LoJack on the car I stole. If your dad likes to put tracking devices on his possessions, and he thinks you're one of them...we may need to check your stuff."

A soft sound of dismay. At once, a deep ache stabs through my chest and I want a chance to hide her in my arms again.

Holding her felt so fucking right that if she wasn't a traumatized virgin recovering from being drugged, I would have seduced her right there. I still want to.

"It's okay," I encourage almost reflexively, my voice going deeper with a hint of desire. "Everything besides your phone is tucked inside a giant metal box right now that serves as a Faraday cage. No tracking signal can get through."

She relaxes. "That makes me feel better. But wouldn't I have found a tracker while I sewed the stash pockets?"

"That makes the most sense. He knew you would

use it if you ever ran away. They have all sorts of designs. It could be in the damn luggage tags."

We've made it to the highway. "Guess we're on our way to Montreal sooner than expected," I sigh. "Anyway, we'll go back and look once I have gotten us a good lead out of town. How much money are you carrying?"

"Twelve forty-thousand-dollar straps of hundreds, plus my Mom's jewelry and all of his." She sounds a little proud, and I laugh.

She's got the makings of a great thief.

"You cleaned him out! Good. Keep your mother's ornaments, though. I can fence his in Montreal if you want."

"Yeah. I don't want anything of his." Her voice is unyielding. She's recovering.

"We have about four and a half hours on I-87. Alas, we'll need to have a layover so a friend can furnish us with the right IDs. He's in Champlain, near the border." The wind picks up, and I fight it for a moment before going on.

"They also ran up on us in the middle of the night, so I'm bushed. I suggest we stop and search your suitcase down the road, and then get some rest."

"Is that safe?" Her voice rises with worry.

"It's safer than driving up to Champlain this late when we're both worn out. And if you pull your bag out of the back before we check it, your dad will know where you are if it's tagged. It's best he doesn't know what city we're hiding out in."

It's more complicated. I can't stand the idea of a live

tracker in the vehicle I call home. Especially since the last of Lucca's trackers most likely had a fucking bomb attached to it.

"That makes sense. And I should probably rest. I still feel kind of sick." She rubs her eyes.

"I have more sports drinks in the back," I reassure her. "Up past Saugerties, there are many back roads in the woods. We can stash the truck there and rest."

"Okay," she murmurs, exhaustion plain in her voice.

It starts to snow thinly as we make our way north. I turn the heater up a notch and put the Stones on low to keep us awake. Beside me, Melissa dozes, only to look up sometimes with a huff, as if she's forgotten where she is.

"So these friends in Montreal, do you know them well?" I'm mostly asking to pass the time, but it would also be nice to know if she's going somewhere safe.

"We've been talking for six months online," she murmurs, staring out the window. "They think I'm running from an ex."

"Close enough. You're not worried they will have second thoughts if they find out who precisely you're running from?" It's a justifiable apprehension.

"I will not be in their hair long enough," she protests...and then goes quiet, probably remembering what happened. "Why?"

"I don't want to hand you off to them and then find out you're stranded." She's been through enough crap.

"Thank you for being so thoughtful. But I trust them. I wouldn't have gotten up the courage to leave without them." And yet...she still sounds troubled.

That's good. I hate being the one to burst her bubble. Internet friends aren't always the people we think they are—not in the catfish sense, but in the day-to-day dependability sense.

"I glad they helped you. Sorry if I seem suspicious, but that's how you stay alive in my line of work." I stifle a yawn as we keep driving.

By the time we pass Saugerties and drive into the mix of forests, ranches, and tiny towns beyond, my head is throbbing, and Melissa is out like a light. She breathes softly as she leans her head against the window. I get off the highway and into one of the winding roads leading through the countryside.

I find us a hollow by a rushing creek, and park under a pine tree that's lightly dusted with snow. I set the brake and parking brake and turn the engine off.

"Hey, wake up, Sleeping Beauty, we're parked. I have an actual bed you can sleep in. Come on."

She stirs, her eyes open, and she gives me a distressed look again—like she's still not used to waking up liberated.

"Oh," she murmurs after taking a moment to sort out what I said. "Good."

I get out to help her into the back. There's just one bed back there, but all I can expect out of our fatigue is a cuddle. That thought alone makes me smile with anticipation.

Chapter 8
Melissa

I wake up to soft breathing beside me and I don't know where I am. The persistent smell of cigars and perfume that permeates my father's house is missing. The pillowcase against my cheek isn't satin but flannel.
We're in the back of Chase's 'escape vehicle.' And the breathing beside me is him.
The unfamiliarity isn't the room or his presence. It's this tentative feeling of safety—of not having to be on guard the moment I wake up—that washes over me like warm water as I look around. It's okay.
I'm down to my silk turtleneck undershirt and fleece-lined leggings I wore under my leathers. I fell asleep before realizing Chase was climbing in behind me.
He didn't even touch me. I hate the idea of him lying awake with a boner all night.

My head is full of damp cotton, and my mouth is dry, but the drug hangover is gone. I roll over and reach for the sports drink on the fold-out nightstand beside me. A few swallows, and the discomfort subsides enough that I can sit up.

I swing my legs off the edge of the bed and set them on the padded floor.

The truck interior is cramped, but livable. The LEDs on the battery powering it blink away on the wall across from me. Beside it is a tiny shower-toilet booth, a floor-to-ceiling cylinder with a funky hatch door.

On the other side is a small counter with a mini-fridge and sink and a single burner stove with a teakettle on it. It's totally uncluttered, so things won't roll around while the vehicle is in motion; the kettle is the only exception right now.

I duck into the bathroom and shut the door to use my phone without the light waking up Chase. The guy's earned his sleep. Not to mention all the cash I promised.

I can't figure out for a few moments why I can't get a signal until I remember: the Faraday cage. The same thing that is keeping me from being traced right now. It's blocking the phone signal.

"Damn." I start scrolling through old messages and calls instead, not playing the voicemails. Most are from Father. He must be furious.

I just don't care anymore. How can I? He's made himself into a scary fiend. There's no room in there for love. Or respect. Or loyalty.

There's always just been fear—and the longing to run away. But I only got the nerve to do so when my father was handing me off to someone even worse. I'll probably have Enzo's family after me, too. Maybe I should petition the Don of Montreal for residence?

Don't really want to stay in Montreal, though. Not even if Dad is petrified of the Sixth Family. He's fearful of certain Russian cartels, too. I check the messages reflexively, get nothing new, of course, and then examine the stored ones. I do have friends in Montreal who care about me. I have the proof right here.

Amelie: Did he hurt u?

Me: Just some bruises. But I need to leave now. I can't wait anymore.

Amelie: He doesn't know about us. Come here! We can put u up for a while until u figure things out.

Me: Are u sure?

Amelie: Yes! It's no trouble at all.

I needed that reassurance. Just a few moments of reading over the old conversation and reminding myself that, yes, people I can rely on await me in Montreal.

I clean myself up in that cramped cylinder, which has a pull-out sink and a steel mirror. Then I open it up as quietly as I can.

Chase is sitting up and blinking at me groggily. "Did you get any rest?"

"Yes," I mutter, trying not to let look at the muscles across his lean belly. How did I manage to sleep next to this amazing hunk and not touch him?

"Okay, good." He slides out of bed and moves past me; the smell of his sweat is mixed with spicy aftershave, and my fingers curl at my sides with the urge to touch him. "Lemme get cleaned up, and I'll make some coffee."
"Great."
I make up the Murphy bed while he's cleaning up. I don't know why I'm doing it exactly: maybe to burn off nervous energy, maybe as a thank you.
There are straps that buckle over the pillows and the top of the bedclothes to secure them when the bed folds into the wall. I tug them into place when he comes out with his hair wet and his skin gleaming faintly from steam.
"Don't worry about that, I'll get it," he tells me cheerfully. He gets the coffee perking and then sets my suitcase on the bed, pulling out his flashlight, knife, and a screwdriver. "He could have put a tracker in this thing before he brought it to you. Wish I had a signal scanner." He takes off the luggage tags first, splits them open with the knife and scrutinizes them. Next, we take out all my clothes and underwear, and I check inside my shoes, socks, and coat for anything thick enough to hide a tiny, hard lump. Lastly, we search the suitcase itself.
"Where did you get the idea to put in these secret compartments?" he asks as he pulls the false backing off its Velcro to expose all the money and jewels tucked in there. I sewed rows of hair ties into the backing, so it could hold stuff without sliding around.
"Stories of smugglers, dinners with mobsters, and I listened really well." I pull my stolen fortune out, putting

the straps of cash on one side and the jewels on the other.

"So you sewed these in ahead of time, planned to steal your dad's stuff on the way out, and then worked on how you would get the chance to get out?" He starts going through the straps of cash, fanning through them and then examining the paper loops holding them together.

"Um, yeah, pretty much. I just kept working at it. I didn't have a plan exactly, because I never knew when the opportunity would come." I used sewing skills from a class to make those secret compartments and learned to crack safes listening to drunken gangsters brag—and talking them into showing off. I got a bodyguard with a crush on me to take me to the gun range 'in case something happens.'

It took a lot of flattery and flirting to get him to cave in—but he did.

I check every inch of the suitcase, and then I start putting back all my clothes while he checks and counts the cash.

"I just...laid the groundwork, and then ran when I had a prospect."

Actually, it was a lucky coincidence. I would have run anyway, even if I would have ended up on the bottom of the harbor.

"I can't blame you." He runs his fingers over one of the straps of cash and frowns, turning it over in his hands.

"He didn't have to threaten. Everyone who crosses or fails him dies." My voice is full of sad inevitability. "Mom, too."

"Holy crap, I'm sorry." He looks up distractedly. "My family was a mess, but never like that."

"Yeah?" I watch him turn that same strap of cash in his hands as if something is different about it. "What did your dad do?"

He gives me a gloomy smirk. "Stepped in front of a bullet that would have hit me. Some crackhead. Totally random."

I stare at him in sympathy and nod, drawn partway out of my own fear and trauma that I'm not alone in carrying grief. "I'm sorry."

Time stretches between us; my cheeks are warm and my stomach is getting fluttery. Is it ordinary to connect with someone this fast?

Do I even know what typical is?

Finally, he drops his gaze back to the strap of cash in his hand. "This one's been reglued," he comments, and then runs his finger under the paper loop to break the seal.

And there it is: on the underside of the printed strap, a single black plastic square with circuitry embedded in it, barely the size of a thumbnail.

"This has to be what they were tracking." And he snaps the chip into pieces before tossing it in the trash. "They can't track you now."

"...Oh." I'm suddenly numb inside. Except he wasn't tracking me! He was tracking his money.

"...Thank you."

That thought sticks in my head as I hand Chase his share of cash and tuck the rest and the jewels back in the suitcase. I'm close to crying as I finish putting everything away. Then I have trouble closing the latch over my folded clothes, and after the suitcase pops open twice I'm suddenly sobbing like a baby—over nothing.

"Oh shit," he mutters, and then he's shutting the suitcase and setting it aside on the floor, and pulling me into his arms. "What is it? What's wrong?"

"I don't know," I cry into his shoulder, clinging to him, glad that someone is here to hold me. All my life, I've held it in. The pain, the fear, the grief, the rage: all of it, hidden, for survival's sake.

But now, away from my father, and with someone safe and kind, and he's holding me against his lean, powerful chest, firmly enough that my heartbeat slows, and I melt against him.

And I cry because I can.

"It'll be okay," he murmurs and grabs a box of tissues before wrapping both arms around me again. He doesn't complain or get impatient or grope me; he's tender. That makes me sob like some deadly poison is leaking out of my tear ducts.

He wipes my tears and brings me water, and rubs my back, and speaks soft reassurances until I pull myself together. I've never met anyone this kind. Maybe it's the whole crazy situation, but what happens next is as unavoidable as the tide.

We kiss.

It's not my first, but the first that didn't leave my lips hurting. His mouth is smooth against mine, his slight stubble scratchy but not unpleasant. He tastes like peppermint gum, and the tip of his tongue teases mine, and I forget how to breathe for a moment.

The kiss ebbs in and out, his lips caressing mine tenderly and then firmly, his arms tightening around me as I slide my hands through his hair. Heat washes over me, a melting sensation that makes me relax and let him do whatever he wants.

His hands start moving over my body, decisively and leisurely, like he's molding my flesh out of clay. They glide up and down my sides, over my arms, my ass, up my back; I start exploring his back and sides with my fingertips, feeling his muscles flex under my touch.

When he breaks the kiss, he looks at me, his eyes smoky behind his eyelashes as they search my face. I'm breathless, bereft, lips still tingling from the kiss and not sure what to say. Then he kisses me again, even more fiercely, and his soft, hungry moan makes my whole body light up with unfamiliar need.

Before, my crush on him was abstract, almost timid. Now, my desire is primal and concrete: I want his body on mine and that big cock deep in my aching pussy. I want to hear him moan and pant and shout my name and to feel his hands all over me just like this—but more.

He starts stroking my breasts through the silk; I gasp and whimper against his mouth as my nipples tighten and electric jolts of sensation run through them. He catches them between thumb and finger and tweaks them, then slides the fabric back and forth over them until my hips start to rock with each stroke.

It's so smooth and comfortable that when he settles me back on the bed, I don't feel nervous at all. I just want more. More kisses, more caresses, more of this lovely tingling that's growing stronger inside of me with every passing moment.

His silk-smoothed hands knead and stroke my breasts almost reverently; he's kissing my neck now, just a little roughly, his breath already ragged. He moves down my body slowly, leaving small, tingling suck marks at my pulse before nuzzling down my neck. When his mouth comes level with my breasts, he buries his nose between them playfully before looking up at me.

I nod, and he slides the silk up to expose me and covers one of my breasts with soft kisses. The teasing soothes and frustrates me at once; his unhurried movements, this tenderness, are what I need—and I moan with relief when his mouth closes over my nipple.

His tongue swirls over my sensitive flesh and then beats against it as he suckles me; I gasp and dig my fingers into his shoulders as he switches to long, luxuriant pulls. I writhe under him, subconsciously grinding my hips, quickly soaking the crotch of my leggings with my juices. "Ah...Chase...don't stop," I beg, and he suckles harder, making me tremble and roll my hips more roughly. The craving to be filled, to be stimulated in ways I barely know about, gets stronger with each stroke. Now his hand's sliding between my legs...and when I mill against it on reflex, he starts rubbing and kneading my hungry kitty beneath the cloth.

"Oh!" I gasp, completely astonished. The sensation is almost perfect...almost exactly what I crave. He finds the top of my labia beneath the wet silk and pinches them closed gently, rubbing them up and down in time with his insistent suckling.

He switches to my other breast; my back arches, and he slips his hand in under my leggings to caress me straightforwardly. He props his smooth thumb against my clit hood and moves it smoothly in time with his mouth; my toes curl and my pussy tightens more with every stroke.

I'm screaming with pleasure now, incandescent with it, burning with it, my voice musical and full of desperation. I can't form words anymore; it feels too good.

And then—

Waves of bliss crash through me, exploding from my contracting cunt and making me gasp and thrash in Chase's grip. It's so good that I want it to last forever...but then the contractions slow and lessen, and finally stop. Satisfied and stunned, I pant for air as I slowly come to my senses.

Chase lifts his head and smiles. "There we go. Did you like that?"

Tears of incredulity fill my eyes. "I came," I gasp, and he nods.

"Yes, you did. And it was stunning." He reaches for the belt of his jeans as I lie there, his impatient cock pushing out the denim. "And now I'd really like to—"

And it's at that exact moment that someone pounds on the back door.

I let out a startled scream and sit up, yanking down my shirt.

"Bathroom," Chase instructs as he straightens, cursing under his breath. "I'll deal with whoever it is."

I slip into the bathroom on wobbly legs, heart beating fast despite my muscles being delightfully relaxed. My skin is covered in sweat, and the scent of my arousal makes me blush as I close the door behind me. I feel like I'm a teenager in a sitcom, hiding in her boyfriend's bathroom while some officious parent bangs on the door. That reminded me of my father, and I freeze, realizing it could be Benny and the others. When I hear the door unlatch and roll up, the first thing through my head is my purse with the gun is outside and a jolt of adrenaline kills my post-orgasmic buzz.

I hear voices. Chase is trying to reason with an unfamiliar man. The conversation is short. Then I hear Chase sigh, and the door rattles closed again. I lighten up—and then he taps on the door.

"Hey, it's a ranger. We can't park here. And no, he won't leave us alone and come back later." His voice is brimming with sexual frustration...and I feel terrible for him.

How many times is it now, twice? And he just showed me what an orgasm feels like.

It was wonderful. And I want more. Damn rangers.

"Um, okay, I'll get dressed," I reply, resenting the interfering ranger. "You'd think he'd have something better to do."

He kisses me, and I feel his still-firm erection press into my belly. "We'll take this back up later," he promises. I'm suddenly breathless and tingly again. "I can't wait."

Chapter 9
Alan

I'm full of conflict as we return to the main highway. It's probably a bad idea to get involved with an escaped mob princess. But damn it...I like her. I don't want to leave her alone in Montreal with strangers.
She would be safer with me.
That's completely irrational. But something about this whole 'friends in Montreal' thing doesn't smell right. Maybe I'm jealous. Maybe I don't want to hand her off to anyone, and I'm just making excuses.
A guy like me can't afford to get attached. I'm always on the road either stealing or transporting. I never stay in one place more than a few seasons.
It means I can't settle down with anyone—unless I find someone willing to wander around with me. If I put

down roots someplace I've been committing crimes, that gives the cops a chance to catch me.

I'd rather shoot myself than end up in jail.

How can Melissa possibly figure into that? She's uprooted now herself. But can she play nomad thief with me? Do I like her enough?

I look at her, staring distractedly out the window with her coppery hair piled haphazardly over her shoulder. The light catches in her eyes, and I feel my chest and the crotch of my jeans go tight. Yeah, I do.

Then again, I know what crisis bonding is. Maybe I should back off until we're safely across the border and not running for our lives.

Then we can talk about it with clear heads. After I've screwed her brains out a few times, anyway. A promise is a promise.

Still, thinking about spending more time with Melissa has left me curious about whether she's even open to the idea. "Hey," I venture, and she turns to me.

"Yeah?" She's smiling, relaxed; there's warmth in her eyes. I focus on the road before I get too distracted. "You, uh...thought about what you want to do once you leave your friends in Montreal?"

She goes quiet for a moment. "I...haven't thought about it. I never got past actually getting to Montreal. That seems weird."

"It doesn't seem weird. When you're in survival mode, you don't think about much beyond what's happening in the next few days. You're trying to get through."

What does she want to do with her life? Will she want to go to college? Learn a new skill? Would she even be interested in a regular job?

She's behind on a lot of things just from being her father's captive. Maybe I can help somehow.

"That's pretty much it. I've been in survival mode for most of my life." Her little laugh at the end of the sentence is humorless.

"It's pretty tough to get asylum in Canada without the right connections," I explain. "You're likely to be booted back into the States. You might just want to make Canada a stopover. It can be a fairly long one, though."

"How long?" She sounds anxious now. I feel bad for making her think about this, but she needs to, and I give enough of a damn to help her get started.

"Six months, using the passports my friend's making for us. Trust me, his stuff will pass muster with officials."

"I believe you." She hesitates for several beats.

"Um...where will you be going after Montreal?"

"I was going to wait the winter out in Lloyd," I started—and caught her flinch out of the corner of my eye.

"I'm sorry—" she starts, the panic in her voice all reflex.

"No, it's okay. I'm not mad. You're paying me half a million dollars, and I don't keep anything personal in my rentals. I don't give a fuck about my deposit."

I reach for her hand as we hit a safe straightaway and feel her skin under my fingers as her panic subsides. "My point is, I don't have plans. So, you know, if things with your friends—"

I don't have the chance to finish my sentence.

One moment, I'm focused on taking the risk and just putting it out there that she can come with me if things don't work out with Amelie and her boyfriend. The next, my guts freeze up, and I say in a serious voice, "Melissa." She goes still.

"Unbuckle your seat belt and get in the foot well. Now." She's down into it and huddled up like a frightened rabbit before I can blink. "Good—now just keep quiet, and don't panic." I take a deep breath, and deal with what I see up ahead.

This stretch of mountainous road, surrounded by forest, is a dead zone for GPS and cellular signals in many spots. It's why I waited until we were in this area before I pulled over to deal with the potential tracker. Unfortunately, I'm not the only one who knows about the dead zone.

Those same goddamned three black cars are waiting almost exactly where it ends. They're lined up at the bottom of the slope where the road widens and a small town breaks the tree line in the distance. Damn it, they must have assumed we were hiding in the dead zone and waited for us!

"What is it?" she gasps.

"They've got the road blocked ahead. They must have figured you'd run for Canada. It's the fastest way out of your father's territory."

"Oh God," she gasps "What do we do?"

"Stay down there and I drive nice and casual. Let's hope they didn't get a glimpse of my truck leaving while they were back in Lloyd. Okay?"

She gulps air and replies shakily, "Okay."

I keep to the speed limit, driving efficiently, ignoring the lump of ice that's forming deep in my guts as we come up on the three sedans. More Crown Victorias. It seems to be a thing with this guy's motor pool.

I hold my breath as we slip past the line of cars. One guy outside the car looks very familiar. Big, round-bellied, weak-chinned, with dark glasses and a cheap black suit. The print of his gun under his jacket is visible from ten yards away.

He looks up as I drive past, and I pray that the difference in my appearance is enough to throw him off. No worries here, everything's perfectly average.

Our truck sweeps past and the cars start to dwindle in my rear camera.

"Is it okay?" she breathes nervously.

"Gimme a sec," I mutter. "I'm not sure yet."

The screech of tires alerts me; I check the rear cam screen and see all three cars behind me. Adrenaline explodes through me. I have to choose now. Bolt or hope it's a coincidence and keep cool?

Then someone leans out of one of the cars and a bullet pings off our fender. "Uh, shit. Nope! Hang on!" And I floor it.

The engine roars as we lunge ahead, and I hear Melissa squeak in surprise as the diesel system that could have towed ten times as much horsepower converts into speed. We fly along the straightaway, widening our lead fast. "Woo! Eat my dust, assholes!"

Ahead the land is heavily shielded by pines. Beyond, the road starts snaking back and forth up into the hills. I'm hoping these bastards don't know the local roads as well as I do. "You all right, sweetheart?" I check in.

"Uh-huh!" she squeaks, voice muffled against her knees.

"Don't worry about them wasting ammo," I shout above the roaring engine. "We're well ahead of the cars, which keep wasting bullets against this truck. It's armored and the tires are puncture-proof. They can't hit you if you just stay down and we keep ahead of them!"

"Okay," she gasps, struggling to calm down. "Okay. Don't want to distract you."

"Good, because I can comfort you or I can save your ass. Not both at one time."

"The second one's just fine!" she squeaks, and it's so cute that I laugh even as I'm trying not to kill us.

One of the LTDs is speeding ahead of the others, accelerating crazily, wheels skidding on the freshly plowed road. It's gaining; I can only go so fast in these conditions, but the maniac behind me doesn't care. Still, I can keep him from passing and getting at me through the windows.

As he comes up on my bumper, I brake-check him smoothly and hear him crush his front grille against the truck's back bumper. His wheels skid—but he keeps control.

"What's going on?" She's sounding calmer. "Should I shoot back?"

"No, stay where you are. Do not pop your head up above the window line. Are you getting knocked around?" What happens if we crash?

"A little."

"Okay, let me see if I can get this guy off of us before we reach the switchback. It's a mile up the road. If I can't, I'll need you to slip into your seat belt, just in case." I'm praying it won't be necessary, but these guys are determined, and my luck hasn't been great lately. Except when it's been amazing, of course—but I can't rely on that.

The guy accelerates and swings over, trying to pass on my right. There's a deep ditch beside the road on that side, half filled with broken branches and snow. I let him creep up on me a foot or two.

Melissa cries out as I cut the wheel over and catch the first LTD by its front end. There's a brutal crunch; wheels skid.

I regain control in a few seconds; we only fishtail once. Then I'm roaring off again with a desperate, uncontrolled screech of tires behind us.

I glance at the rear-view mirror and see the LTD go into the ditch, rear end flying up in a rooster-tail of snow. One of the other cars skids out as they try to slow down and stop to check on their buddy. The other accelerates again and comes after us.

"Damn. One's still stuck to us. Okay, buckle up."

She springs out of the foot well and into her seat, buckling the harness around her with trembling hands as I keep ahead of the LTD. There isn't enough straightaway left to pull the same trick twice; besides, they're hanging back now, trying to shoot out my tires instead.

"There's a pretty sharp turn ahead. I have to pull a trick to get us through at this speed. If I mess up, I can roll us.

Stay as calm and possible and do not distract me by screaming. Okay?" I can't keep the tension out of my voice anymore.

"Okay." She covers her face with her hands, and I focus on the road. "I trust you." It sounds like she's convincing herself.

Which I can't take personally under the circumstances.

I have to time this perfectly. The truck has a higher center of gravity than is ideal for a trick like this at this speed. I have to compensate with skill—skill I'm trusting the guy behind me does not have.

Besides, I know a curve is there. I'm betting that he doesn't.

Everything seems to slow down as my reflexes kick in. I've done trucks twice this size in curves like this to win bets, and I've come through with dents. Now my hands and feet almost move on their own: the truck becomes my body.

The tires scream as it drifts around the turn, the back end swinging out too far; I correct just in time and make it. For a moment, I'm fighting to straighten out, then the turn is behind me.

A second later, the LTD plows through the curve sideways and slams into a big pine with a sickening crunch. And only then, when that sound hits our ears, does Melissa finally let out a startled cry.

I straighten out fully and slow down enough to take the turns ahead at a sane speed. My heart's beating fast, and I have to ease my grip on the steering wheel. "You all right?"

"Are they still after us?" I check the rear-view and see nothing on the road but scattered debris.

"I think they stopped to peel their guys out of those two wrecks before the police get here."

A huge wave of relief washes over me and I let out a laugh. "Holy crap, that was too much. Bet you're glad you hired me now, huh?" I flash a grin at her that is less cocky and more just full of happiness that we came through.

"More than ever," she sighs. "Do you think they know we're heading to Canada?"

"It's a good bet. We better get off 87 in case they try to set up another ambush." I hear the relief strong in my voice.

"Damn. How do we keep them from grabbing us at the border?" She's sounds worried again.

"I know the roads better than them," I reply confidently. "There are a lot of roads near the border where you can literally end up on Canadian soil by mistake. They're not the best roads, especially in winter, but once we have our papers, nobody's going to care if they find us driving around there."

"And if the back roads are closed?"

"There are a few smaller checkpoints. He can't watch them all; they're not even in his territory if I remember correctly." Still no sign of any pursuit. I start to calm down.

"Yeah, that's the Don of Montreal's border. He controls it, not my father. Part of why I picked it." She sits there thoughtfully for a moment. "They don't search the truck or anything?"

"Not unless you do something to make them suspicious. They just have you answer questions and check your passport." I think about it as we weave our way up through the mountains. "We'll have to disguise ourselves, though."

She looks at me curiously. "Disguise? Really?"

My smile is tinged with mischief. "Yeah, we need to make a few stops before we go to the photo studio. Believe me, it'll be worth it. By the time my guy's done, we'll both have new looks and a new identity."

Intermission

Carolyn

"Tell me how your subject managed to escape Lloyd in the middle of the night?" my boss is demanding as I stifle a yawn. It's been a wild night—and his anger is the least of my concerns.

"Short form? He was chased out of town by a three-vehicle of New York City mobsters looking for the girl he's with." I'm so sick of David's shit at this point that I don't much care what he thinks of my casual tone. It's six in the morning, and I spent most of the night in the freezing rain.

"What? Okay, fill me in." His anger subsides as he smells an interesting story. David is like a big kid; if I can keep him entertained and keep from bruising his ego too deeply, I can usually get him off my back for a while.

"I was casing Chase's rental as suggested." More like freezing to death on a parking structure doing on-the-fly research on the girl he was with. "He arrived home at

2:45, accompanied by a woman I positively identified as Melissa Lucca."

"The mob princess? Gianni Lucca's daughter?"

"Correction." I can't keep the glee out of my voice. "Gianni Lucca's runaway daughter trying to get away from him. Who probably has a lot of evidence against him and is likely to make a deal to get rid of him."

"Fuck!" He breathes heavily; I can imagine him pacing in a small circle in his office. "That's too good a lead not to chase, and you're the only one in position."

I want to laugh at him. "Yes, sir."

"All right." He pauses to think. It probably takes him a lot of effort. "We know this guy has done transports before. Does he have ties with the Lucca's?"

"No. My guess is, she hired him as a freelancer." Actually, I know she did. I just don't know how—nor who exactly sent me the information about it.

The texts came last night from what was probably a burner phone, which blocked me as soon as I tried to text back.

Right after I saw Alan Chase's imposing boner and dropped my damn binoculars over the edge of the parking structure. Apparently the guy didn't just take the job with Melissa for the money.

Lucky girl. He's not my type, but...damn.

The set of texts set my alarm bells off from the very first line. But they also supplied accurate—and very important—information when I verified.

Pay very close attention, Special Agent, or an innocent woman is going to die.

The Lucca family's only daughter Melissa is with Mr. Chase.
She is seeking to escape. I want you to help her.
Enforcers are coming to collect or kill her. Look for a trio of black Crown Victorias.
Warn Mr. Chase in any way possible.
Whoever it was ignored my requests to identify themselves. In conclusion, I did as instructed—and quickly saw the cars drive off the highway in a tight line and head toward the house I was watching. I got the inhabitants' attention with my flashlight and watched through my telephoto lens as they ran.
Who sent that message? I have a few suspicions, but nothing concrete enough. And until I know, I'm not giving up this new source to David quite yet.
"Will you let me take this on the road, or do I stay posted in Lloyd and wait for further instructions?" Right now, the paperwork's keeping me in place. There's only so much non-cooperation of the boss I'm willing to risk at one time.
"Absolutely get on the road. Any idea where they're headed?" He's typing swiftly in the background now.
"North. It has to be. It's the fastest way out of Lucca territory." I have mixed feelings about handing a frightened, innocent witness like Melissa Lucca over to David. But if I can get my name connected to a win as high-profile as bringing down her father, I won't be chasing down the slippery perps on David's never-been-caught list anymore.

"North. Okay. I'll get the Buffalo field office to send some backup and see if they can look for her at the border. We'll let the RCMP know, too." More typing. Then, almost grudgingly: "Good job."

"Thank you, sir." Yeah, you better distinguish me after putting me through all this shit.

But it still leaves me wondering: who is my mystery informant, and how did they know? How did they know where to reach me?

Maybe it's a mobster Melissa got to help her? Maybe it's Melissa? Or maybe it's...someone else?

I glance over at the folder sitting on the corner of my desk warily, as if it contains a poisonous snake. There's another possibility—another person who could get information like myself with little effort.

I'm not ready to open that folder, go to my fifth suspect, and contemplate that possibility. There's no way he's involved. The nation's most notorious unrestrained hacker wouldn't care about some girl escaping from her dreadful family.

Or would he?

"All right, I'm giving you extra for the travel budget and lodging near the border. I'll call you back with specifics. Start packing." His tone is curt and reluctant, but I'm smiling anyway.

Chasing one of the slipperiest car thieves in the US isn't my idea of a good use of my time. But helping a terrified girl escape from a father who wants her captive or dead—and taking a step toward putting him behind bars—making my bones with the FBI in the process? That's more my speed.

My phone buzzes again. It's another unfamiliar phone number.

There's been a crash on 87.

Lucca's men. Two of the three cars are out of commission.

He will send reinforcements. Expect them at the border.

"Oh, that's going to be fun," I mutter sarcastically, thinking of a giant border mess of FBI, RCMP, and mobsters waiting for Chase and Melissa.

Who are you? I text my mystery informant.

Be patient, Special Agent.

Your cooperation will lead to my being more forthcoming.

And then they cut me off again. "Shit," I growl, and then get up to stomp around my hotel room and pack.

I have to get to Melissa and Alan Chase before they reach the border or this could go haywire very fast.

Chapter 10
Melissa

"I don't want to cut my hair or dye it," I admit as we pull up in front of the hairdresser. The city where the forger lives is a small, desolate place, windswept and snowy. Next to Lloyd, which nestles close to Poughkeepsie and is a short drive from the city, this town feels as remote as an Alaskan outpost.

"I don't want you to either—your hair is wonderful." He parks, then leans over and nuzzles my hair briefly as I giggle. "But it's also distinguishing, and you have some frightful people looking for you."

"I understand. It's just..." My hair is the only thing I inherited from my mother—besides her horrible situation. Everyone in my dad's family is darker with hair the color of coffee. Being the token redhead always felt like a mutiny.

"It won't be forever. Maybe get a weave so you can change the length without cutting anything off?" He leans back and unfastens his seat belt. He's already changed his hair by cropping it almost military short, disappointing me. I wanted to run my fingers through it again.

"That's a pretty good idea," I muse. A wig isn't feasible; if I'm searched, it will raise questions. I want to change back to my old hair without waiting for it to grow out. The hairdresser is a minute old woman who chatters amiably and clucks at Chase for not putting a ring on my finger yet. She makes me chuckle as she turns my strawberry blonde locks into a straight, dark auburn braid. The unfamiliar weight tugs at my scalp as I look at myself in the mirror.

"It brings out your eyes," Chase reassures as he steps in beside me and kisses my cheek. "Now, let's get you a change of clothes."

By the time we pull up in front of the converted barn outside town, we look like a completely different couple. I've traded my leathers for wool: a herringbone jacket over a smart pantsuit in dark aubergine. A pair of dark-rimmed glasses sit on my nose.

"I'm digging the sexy librarian look," Chase encourages. I'm trying to ignore how hot he looks in his dark tweed suit. If I don't, I'll be too tempted to suggest we climb into the back of his conversion truck again.

"It's not me. But...I suppose that's the point." Nobody in my family would recognize me. I look out of the ordinary: professional and confident.

When we walk up to the property, a security camera swivels to fix on us, and a voice speaks through the grille by the door. "You got the cash, Chase?" rasps a smokers' voice so croaky I can't figure out if it's male or female. "Aw, come on, Paulie, would I come to you empty-handed?" Chase grins up at the camera. "It's all here. Open up."

"All right, give me a minute," the voice grumps. A chair creaks and the intercom crackles again.

Whoever is behind the door buzzes us in; a heavy-sounding lock clunks, and Chase steps forward to push the door open. The air that rushes out is warm and smells heavily of cigarette smoke. I stifle a cough as I follow Chase inside.

The entryway is a completely walled off room lined in cheap wood paneling. It looks like a photography studio, if a bit more cluttered and stinky. I turn and give Chase a dubious look, but he smiles and pats me on the back.

"It doesn't look like much, but trust me. Paulie's the best and he works fast."

I don't have time to speak before the unlabeled steel door behind the counter opens, and a small, skeletal man who looks like an aging rocker bounces through the door and walks up to us.

Yellow stains on his lips and fingers, his shirt has burn holes and so do his jeans, and he smiles at us with outsized yellow teeth. "How's it going? That's a new look for you, and who's the girl? I'm Paulie. Hi."

I just sort of blink at him. "...uh. Hi."

His seamed hand shoots out and I shake it, coughing from the cigarette fumes coming off of him. He just keeps on talking.

"Pleasetameetcha. Look, uh, Alan, I got to know what names to put on this. You guys passing as a married couple?"

"Yeah," Chase says easily, and I nod. "Eric and Madelyne Corso."

It took us a while to settle on names, but with the demolition derby in the mountains behind us, we had nothing but time on the road. Time to plan, flirt, talk about maybe spending some time together in Montreal. I'm glad he'll be sticking around, at least for a while.

I don't want to go without his touch again.

How to introduce him to my friends in Montreal? There's so much craziness going on! Falling for someone unexpectedly is a welcome bright note in the middle of it. Would they understand?

They probably wouldn't comprehend the fake ID to get across the border safely. Or the rest of it, for that matter. The extent of their problems is just that they are perpetually broke—something I plan to help them with.

"That's cute, you're a charming couple." Paulie bobs his head, his stringy gray hair clinging to the sides of his narrow face. "Okay! So. I'm going to get your photos, set up the documentation, put your passports together, and then you're out of here."

Chase sighs. "There's something else, Paulie. I need you to babysit my truck for a week or so."

"Oh, you're taking the Mercedes? All right." He digs in the pocket of his ratty jeans for his keys, then pulls one off the ring and hands it over. "Got her repainted in a nice neutral blue, like you asked. Shouldn't stick out at all."

"Thanks." He counts off several hundreds from his wad and hands them over. "That cover everything?"

Paulie checks briefly. "Yeah, thanks, I hate asking."

Chase nods. "I remember." He turns to me. "You want to get your photos done first?"

***

My head is pounding from a couple of hours of that smoky air once we get out of the photo studio with our new passports and car registration. Paulie was brilliant, but hard to breathe around. "I need to take a walk or something after that."

"Yeah, me, too." We get my suitcase out of the truck and he secures everything before we drive it around to the back of the barn. The blue Mercedes SUV is waiting for us; it blends in completely with what the richer set drives Upstate.

We put my stuff in the back of the Mercedes and then take a slow walk around the stubbled field nearby. Occasional flakes drift down; our breath steams and the frozen mud feels rubbery under my boots. "We know almost nothing about each other," Chase starts, and I feel myself tense.

"Yes. This started out as business," I venture, still wondering what it is now. It feels like it's starting to be a romance. But what do I know about that?

"Yeah. Not any longer. You and I know it." The thin snow crunches under our boots as we walk speechless for a while.

"If we stuck together after Montreal—" I start, and then freeze, my own daring and impulsiveness confusing me. He shoots me a glance and then looks away, hands digging deeper into his pockets. "Let me guess. You're going to say that it's too dangerous for me to be paired off with you, because you're always going to be running from your father."

He's right—that's what has to be brought up. "That's part of it, yeah."

"What's the rest, then? Because I'm used to running. I'm good at it. That makes it difficult for anyone to catch you."

I trudge alongside him, digging for the right thing to say. "I...have problems, Chase. Being in that place with those people messed me up pretty bad. You saved me, and one of the first things I did was pull a gun on you. I know that's not typical."

He lets out a sharp laugh. "No, it's not, but nothing about that situation was ordinary. I can't blame you for an intense response to fucked-up circumstances."

"Oh." We keep walking. A couple of jays follow us curiously from tree to tree. "So."

"So maybe..." he ventures. "Maybe call off your meeting with the friends you've never actually met, and go with me instead?"

I stop and look at him, my breath catching in my throat. "...What?"

"We could head for British Columbia and stay there for a while. The weather's better, the people are nice, the weed's legal, and the beer's good." He's talking faster, his eyes alight, and deep inside something feels unmoored, as if this is a dream.

"I...should really...at least check in with them," I manage. Neither seems right. "They've worried for me for months, I should at least...say hello."

He seems relieved. "Well, that's not a no."

I smile then, and a warmth inside me dispels more of my grief and alarm. "No, it isn't. I have a promise to keep."

"Those are important." We're halfway around the pasture fence now, turning to walk back. A few flakes fall into my hair, and he reaches up to brush them away.

I take in a shivery breath. "This is a weird way to meet someone, you're right. My whole life's been weird. I...don't want to walk away from you when we get to Montreal."

He stops me tenderly, moving in front of me and picking my chin up to look at him with a feather-light touch. "I don't want to walk away. Don't know where this is going, but right now I want you with me."

I smile softly. "Okay."

His kiss gives me another foreign feeling: gratification. For a moment, there in his arms, it's enough just to be there. Not dwelling on the past, not fearing the future. Right now, I'm alive, and with him, and that's enough.

Chapter 11
Alan

I'm terrible. After a tender moment like that, all I can think of is fucking.

Still, we're less than two hours away from ending this voyage—and after that, there's plenty of time to consummate the relationship. My blue balls have been practically exploding since I met her: so damn many hesitations and interruptions. That's almost over.

I just have to be patient.

Crossing into Canada is more intricate than expected, simply because many of the back roads are closed for the winter. We settle for the crossing at Trout River, far enough away from 87. It takes about half an hour extra to get there, but we spend it well, talking about the best kind of nothing.

"Favorite food?" I ask her as we ease down a slushy road that hasn't been plowed in three days.

"Cheeseburgers." She's looking everywhere now, eyes wide and wondering, like a kid on their first road trip. "With dill pickles and a lot of cheddar cheese."

"Really? Is there a story behind that?" The station is in the distance; there's a whole lot of nothing and you can see for miles.

"This bodyguard had a crush on me back when I was sixteen." Her smile is strained for just a moment. "He never touched me, but he wanted to.

"I was trying to learn to defend myself, but my dad would never get behind it. I asked Tony to start taking me to the range to learn to shoot. It took a lot of persuading, but I got him to take me and teach me the basics." She glances at her handbag, and I do, too—I've never been able to forget she has a gun in there.

"That reminds me, close up your purse. They won't search you going through the checkpoint, but if they discover it when we're handing over our passports, we'll be in trouble." Although not many uniforms give trouble to observably well-to-do couples.

That's why the conservative clothes, the tweed, the dark Mercedes; not only were our appearances disguised, but also our origins. We're making the crossing in the guise of newlyweds on a trip to Montreal for New Years and a movie festival.

"No problem." She pulls out her passport and closes her purse, setting it down in the foot well. "Anyway, so every time after a lesson we had a 'date' in the local Five Guys.

I really like their burgers. Every time I ate one, I was doing something Father wouldn't approve of."

I chuckle and nod. My own food preferences are simpler: they're a family tradition. "I like barbecue. I am really picky and not the best cook." I slow down to drive around another mound of snow. I'm now glad we couldn't bring the truck—maneuvering it in this mess would have driven me crazy.

"My dad was really good at barbecuing." I'd rather not think about that. "I just don't have the talent."

"I don't know if I do. My mom wasn't around, and none of father's female relatives wanted to stick around him." She gives a sad snicker. "Can't blame them, but nobody was around to teach me stuff like cooking."

"How do you look so put together then?" I don't know a damn thing about how women teach each other. Grandpa raised me alone.

"Father sent me to classes. You know, finishing school. He always thought of marrying me to somebody too rich to care if I could do anything practical." Her gaze goes distant. "Maybe I would be good at it."

"Do you know how to drive?" I ask as we draw nearer to the checkpoint. Just keeping the dialogue on mundane things—distracting her from any fretting about the crossing.

"Not really. I was trying to get Tony to teach me when father decided to marry me off. After that he had me on lockdown."

"I can teach you if you want. It takes practice, but once the movements become your reflexes, you barely think about it. Unless, of course, you end up driving professionally."

We get in line behind a red Jetta with neon snowboards mounted on the hood. Not many people crossing the border this afternoon.

"I'd like that," she says dreamily, checking her phone.

"Trying to call your friends again?" She's been trying off and on since we got near the border. Each time, her troubled frown deepened.

"Yeah, I keep getting their answering service. They asked me to call when I was an hour away, but now they're not picking up."

"Don't worry about it. We can go by and knock on the door, and if nobody answers, we'll get a room, go out to eat, and worry about it later. You're not depending on them for a place to stay." With so much money, she can easily check into a hotel.

But if I wasn't here, she would have been petrified in a big city like Montreal with no experience in fending for herself. That makes me more relieved I am here with her.

She nods, unclenching her hands. "You're right. We have time."

"Yeah." I want to take up that time with things a lot more pleasant than dealing with a slightly questionable couple, but...I understand her need to settle her mind.

"You know, a lot is going on that I don't know much about. But I'm doubly relieved we went for disguises and a change of cars."

"Do you think my father's got guys watching each of the entry points?" She peers over her glasses at the road ahead, probably on the lookout for black sedans.

"He might try. Or he might bribe them to look for us. And I still wonder who the person on top of the parking structure figures into this.

"We'll be okay either way. We're going as a couple, in disguise, with damn good paperwork, and a car that most thieves would sell as soon as they got their hands on it." I reach over and squeeze her hand.

"It's smartest to presume we'll make it through," she mumbles timidly, and I nod.

"Think about what we'll do in Montreal once we get there. Don't agonize over the checkpoint. We'll go through it, they'll ask questions about fruit, and we'll be on our way."

I've been across the border to Canada and Mexico so many times that I almost have the routine memorized. What to do, what not to do, how to dress, what to drive. What red flags they're looking for. What happens if they search the car.

Right now, I'm hiding how apprehensive I am about them taking us aside for a search.

The gun will sink us. And if the border guards have been bribed, or his men are watching, she'll be back in her father's hands by sunset.

"It'll be fine," I say again, and can't tell if it's for her or for me.

Chapter 12
Melissa

Chase is tenser than he seems to want to let on. He's holding it in for me, so I play along and calm myself with some chatter.
"Maybe we should actually go to the film festival. You got those tickets already and I've never been to one." I frown as I realize something. "I've never been to the movies at all. Not in a theater."
"We can absolutely fix that." He puts his hand back on the steering wheel. "It's not as fun as it used to be. You certainly couldn't get in with a gun in your purse."
"I don't want to get into the habit of carrying this thing." I look at my purse; the end of the gun's grip pushes the lavender leather out slightly. I nervously push it under the seat with my feet.

"You're just keeping it for protection, I know, but guns bother the hell out of me." He takes an unsteady breath. "Too many bad memories."

"I don't want that in my life. If you can do without a gun, then I can survive on my own without one, too." I really don't want to make him uncomfortable. He's sacrificed so much for my comfort already—including two chances to fuck me.

We pull forward. My heart's beating fast. I ignore it, folding my hands around the passport on my lap.

"I'll take you to a nice restaurant after we see your friends. I've certainly got the cash." He flashes a grin, apparently thinking nothing of turning around and spending some of his payment on me.

That makes me smile. Where on the road did we go from 'me' to 'us'? But I take comfort in it.

Especially once we come up to the window and are looking a pair of calm, ordinary border agents in the face.

"Any food, fruit, vegetables or plants?" one asks while barely looking up. The other is silent, but looks intently between us, as if memorizing our faces.

"None of the above," Chase says coolly while I try not to squirm under the silent man's gaze.

His partner asks a few more questions like souvenirs of unsealed wood, any animal hides, any drugs, and any weapons. When he asks about the weapons, it takes all my self-control to keep my eyes on my hands. We hand over our passports—and each receive a stamp; they get handed back and we're waved through.

And just like that, I'm across the border, and out of my father's territory! This area belongs to the Don of Montreal, and he utterly hates my father. Which is why I picked his territory. The fact that someone could put me up for a while there was an added motivation.

And now I don't even need that.

"Whew! See? No problem!" Chase steers the car onto the highway beyond the checkpoint and we take off, carefully keeping under the speed limit. "How are you doing?"

I wipe my eyes. "I'm free! I got away!"

His grin widens. "You did! Now let's go see your friends."

Marcel and Amelie have a small apartment in Griffintown in a brick building that sits next to a park. My stomach flutters as we pull up outside. What am I going to tell them when I introduce Chase?

And yet...a fresh wave of relief washes over me as I get out. This is it: the finish line. Once I knock on that door, my journey's finished.

"I can't believe we're actually here," I burble.

"Hey, give me some credit. I wasn't about to let you down." His voice is gently teasing, but I blush.

"I don't mean it like that. I'm still shocked every time I wake up, and it's not in my bed at my father's mansion." I glance his way and feel the prickling in my cheeks ease up at his sympathetic look.

"Oh. I get that. I mean, as much as I can. Should I stay here?" He's carefully looking around as he speaks, scoping out the street, the parked cars, and the few people walking around.

"I don't know." I hesitate. "Maybe I should talk to them and make sure they're all right with an extra guest? And to let them know we're not staying. It's going to look bad if I show up with a suitcase and a new boyfriend."

He lets out a laugh. "Okay. Give me a ring when you've sorted things out. I'm going to get some coffee at that shop we passed on the corner."

I leave my suitcase in the Mercedes. I'm not worried about Chase making off with the last of my money. I've come to trust him as much as Amelie. More—and in an even shorter time.

We kiss before parting, and it's full of heat: promises for later.

Then up the stairs I go.

I feel my step getting lighter, my purse bouncing against my hip as I hurry up the stairs. The damn gun is still in there. Don't open the purse until I'm back in the SUV! The last thing I need is to scare people who were willing to take me in sight unseen.

After climbing some stairs and taking a wrong turn in the maze-like halls I find their apartment. My heart's beating fast as I knock on the door. I hear a rustle and conversation inside, and then someone walks for the door.

Oh good, they're home. Why didn't they pick up?

I have a million things in my head as the door unlatches: thanks, apologies, explanations, giving credit for being a beacon of hope when I had no one. I haven't even set eyes on Amelie or Marcel yet, and they're already the best friends I have ever had. When the door swings open, I'm happy, relaxed, and hopeful.

But then I see my father standing in the doorway.

I freeze, even as a voice in the back of my head screams for me to run. There is no scenario in my mind that allows for my father's smirking presence as he reaches out to seize my wrist. The best I can manage is one harsh scream before he pulls me inside.

"There you are, you little bitch." His heavy palm strikes the side of my face and knocks me to the floor; he lets me fall and I land just inches from someone else's wingtips. "Do you know what kind of trouble you've caused me?"

Terror rolls through me like a storm. I shiver, and feel the urge to plead, lie, explain, and do anything to keep him from killing me. But I know it won't help; it didn't help Mom, either. He'll beat me and maybe even shoot me no matter what I say.

I screamed; someone must have heard. This isn't Lucca's town. And Chase was probably in earshot.

Hold out and hope someone comes!

I keep quiet instead. Benny is sitting there on a scruffy couch with no expression on his face. His gun is out, and it's pointing sideways, his arm casually resting on his lap. It's not pointing at me.

I turn and see Marcel and Amelie sitting stiffly on the far end of the couch, like frightened kids. Not tied up, saying nothing, and facing forward—with their eyes wide and looking at me.

The fact that their hands aren't tied tells me more than I want to know. It tells me the gun's a just-in-case. It tells me something that hurts far worse than the kick to my back that knocks my chin against the floor.

I look up with my bitten lip stinging and fresh blood trickling down one side of my chin, and I demand of my so-called friends, "What did you do?"

Amelie's eyes widen further and she looks away, pretending she didn't hear. Marcel's face is as blank as Benny's.

That infuriates me; shock, sadness, fear, and betrayal are burned away in a blast of fire. Before I can say anything more, my father aims another kick to my ribs, and I'm balling up to protect myself.

Balling up around my purse and the gun inside.

I start struggling to pull the zipper open as I'm being kicked. The beating is not even powerful; it's meant to cause more pain than injury: a spanking—by my father's standards.

If I can just get enough chance between blows to pull Benny's gun out and roll over, I'll blow my father's brains all over the wall.

"Get her phone; she's trying to go for it," my father says in a bored voice, and Benny grabs my purse by the strap and gives it a yank.

"No!" I tighten my body around the purse, hanging onto it with all my strength, and the strap breaks.

"Damn it." Benny gets up. "Come on, sweetheart, you've always been a good girl. Give up the damn purse. Don't make us really hurt you."

"You're going to hand me off to a fucking rapist after killing my mother, and you want to tell me to be a good girl?" I spit blood on Amelie's unpadded wool rug as she lets out a small cry of consternation.

I shoot her a savage look. Oh, now you have something to say, huh?

How could I be so wrong? Am I the worst judge of character because I've been around monsters my whole life?

Am I wrong about Chase, too?

Maybe he isn't coming. Maybe nobody is.

Despair crashes down on me like my father's polished shoe on my back, smothering my defiance and my anger.

"Running up to Canada with some guy, huh? You better still be a virgin when I hand you over to Enzo, you little slut!"

I hear it, and every word digs deeper into my heart. My monster father has me. My friends have betrayed me. Chase is gone.

I'm alone.

But...wait. Does that mean I stop fighting? Especially since I could be about to die?

I close my eyes...and then with my last flicker of free will, yank the zipper on my purse.

My hand darts into the gap as I roll over, and there's father looming above me like so many times before—but his smug look dissolves as he sees my face.

I don't even pull the pistol from the purse when my hands close around the grip; I just flick the safety off.

The steel toe of my boot slams upward into his balls just before I pull the trigger.

Amelie screams; Marcel starts babbling in French. I know I'm screaming something, too, some jumble of obscenities in Italian and English, but my ears are ringing, and everything seems far off.

The look on his face is worth any pain; I shoot him twice in the chest, and he hits the floor at my feet. I sit up, aiming at his head this time—and something hard and heavy clouts me across the back of my skull, sending me into darkness.

Chapter 13
Alan

I hear a commotion down the street as I slip into the crowded coffee shop, but I'm immediately preoccupied when a kid with a coffee tray runs into me and spills half of a latte on my coat.
"Oh, shit, sorry man, my bad," he says, grabbing napkins off the molded cardboard tray and mopping my front clumsily.
"Yeah, no problem, 'scuse me," I grumble, feeling my temper flare, but unwilling to get into it with some poor dope whose biggest offense was not paying attention.
I get my coffee and croissant and sit down at a tiny round table in one corner of the packed room. I'm barely settling in and have my first bite of flaky goodness in my mouth, when someone steps out of the crowd and sits down across from me.

"Uh, hi," I say in mild puzzlement. The woman's in her early thirties maybe, tall and striking, with a white-blond braid coiled at the back of her neck. "Can I help you with something?"

"No, but I think I can help you, Mr. Alan Chase." Her voice is low and calm, with a faint Georgia accent.

My eyebrows go up. "Who the hell are you?" I ask, more dumbfounded than hostile.

"Special Agent Carolyn Steele," she says in a conversational tone, and my guts knot up.

"You're out of your jurisdiction, Special Agent," I point out, and she nods.

"I'm well aware. And I'm not here for you, anyway." Her voice stays low and calm.

I take a swallow of my coffee as I look her over. She looks tired, but focused. Her underarm holster prints slightly against her suit jacket as she leans toward me and offers a brief look at her badge. From what I can see, she's legit.

That could make problems for me back home. I better hear her out.

"Fine, why are you here?" My thoughts are racing; something's up. I suddenly regret leaving Melissa behind to meet with her friends alone.

"Because Gianni Lucca is in Montreal."

Ice runs up my back. Melissa. I start to get up. "I have to go."

"Wait." Her hand shoots out and grabs my wrist with surprising strength. "If you run to your girlfriend's rescue with no plan and no help, all you'll get is a bullet."

I sit down slowly, staring at her. "How do you know about our situation?"

She draws her hand back. "We've been watching you in Lloyd for over a month."

It takes me a moment to get past my surprise. I was right on the brink of being caught by the FBI? But instead of catching me, she helped me.

I put two and two together. "You're the person with the flashlight? On the parking structure?"

"Yeah, that's me. Glad I got your attention. I had no idea you changed jobs to help runaways." She checks her phone screen.

"And you followed me to the border."

"Yes." Her tone is calm and matter-of-fact. "Not directly, but we had border security keeping an eye out for you. Not a bad disguise, but I've been studying you too long to be fooled."

If she's been watching me that long and hasn't hauled me in, it's because she's never actually caught me in a job. This technically is not illegal. The gun and the passports, however, are, and that makes me wary.

"Colored contacts irritate my eyes." I stare at her. "What's your angle?"

"It's very simple. I was assigned to watch you until you slipped up. Then you went and did something that wasn't criminal at all, but downright heroic. And doing it flushed Lucca into the open in pursuit of his daughter." She watches my face as I realize.

"You're after Lucca."

"That's right. Now, I can't do anything north of the border but alert the local authorities. Find a way to send him to his territory, and we can grab him at the border." Her eyes gleam conspiratorially.

If that happens, Melissa doesn't have to run scared anymore. First I have to get her away from her father.

"Tell me what you're offering if I help scare Lucca out of Quebec?"

"Help rescuing your girlfriend. And I'll look the other way when you return to the US." Her gaze is rock-steady. If she's lying, she's the smoothest liar in the world.

"Why not just grab Lucca when he brings her to the border and leave me out of it?" Why is this agent is involving her?

She hesitates. "It's not only about grabbing Lucca. Melissa can't stay in his hands that long. For one thing, she'll instantly become a hostage. And that's not all."

"What then?"

"When I found out who that girl is, I knew right away what she was trying to do. We've known Lucca since his wife's body washed up on the Jersey shore twenty years ago. The man is a fiend.

"Think what you want about law enforcement, but I didn't work for the damn badge so I could let guys like Lucca do whatever they want." She watches my face vigilantly.

"So you helped cover our escape, and you offer even more help now because...why? Because of Melissa?" I don't believe in idealist cops. Especially ones past thirty. "Out of the kindness of your heart?"

"No," she replies, her tone so grim and with so much anger under the surface it startles me. "Because I used to be Melissa."

I sit back, taken by surprise at her sudden passion. She's not being literal. But in the way she physically draws herself up tightly, the tough cop suddenly wrestling with some hideous memory, I get it.

"Seems a lot of women deal with that." It only adds to my anger. I never conceived being that kind of guy, and no man in my family would either. Abusive dads are out there...and in one damn weekend I've met two women disturbed by them.

"It's the sisterhood nobody wants to be in," she sighs, looking away. "And it's bigger than anybody wants to believe."

It's that raw vulnerability that sways me.

That and my lack of options. Because I will not let Melissa stay in her father's hands.

"Fine," I swallow my coffee down and leave the croissant with the one bite on my plate. "We walk, you talk. I'm not leaving her in his hands one second longer."

The snow is drifting down again as we walk back; she talks quickly, hands shoved into her pockets. "The apartment is under surveillance. They have her and the two residents hostage. Two men are in the apartment including her father, and four men in the sedans out back."

"Are they parked within view of the apartment?" I'm fighting to think past my rage. This is the second time that I have wanted to kill someone—just gun them down. It's not a good feeling.

"No, they're communicating via cellular. I can temporarily jam their signals, but that still leaves four armed men." She looks at me. "Do you have a gun?"

"If you know me, you should know I don't carry." I can't keep the edginess out of my voice. "If you block their signals and hold anybody left at gunpoint, I can fabricate a distraction to get the last two outside."

"That will take something pretty dramatic. Not a gunfight, I hope?"

I shake my head, smiling grimly. My mind returns to the night I rescued Melissa. That LTD reminded me so much of my own that had been t-boned.

"No. A car crash."

Chapter 14
Melissa

I awake to tied hands, dried blood on my chin, and my father's laughter.

My father is still alive! I shot him, kicked him, and he's well enough to laugh. Dizzy, head throbbing, every place he hit me is an aching bruise, and for a moment I wonder if he really is an evil spirit and simply can't be killed.

I'm on the couch and Amelie and Marcel are still obediently huddled on the other end. Benny is seated in a chair next to me. My father is leering from across the room.

"I shot you," I manage after a moment. "How the hell are you alive?"

He's pale, bathed in sweat, with little spots of color on his cheeks and the end of his nose. He has a bottle in his hand—not a tumbler with one of those Japanese ice balls he likes so much, but a half-empty fifth with the cap missing. His tie and jacket are off.

"Yeah, you shot me, and I got to admit, I'm impressed." He lounges in his seat smirking, eyes little crescents of amusement. "Kind of poignant. The only kid I got with any balls is a daughter!"

At my silent stare, he laughs again and unbuttons his shirt. A throat strap of a white bullet-proof vest is visible. My heart sinks. "I should have shot you in the face instead!"

"That was your mistake, and you won't get a chance to make it twice." His tone goes hard.

Marcel, at last, speaks up. "Please, you have her now. Can you just give us the money and go? I had to tell the neighbors the television was up too loud."

That confirms it. "You set me up, you fucking slime!" I spit at Marcel, and he looks away, as if I just slapped him.

"Oh, don't blame Marcel there," Benny speaks up, fishing in his pocket to pull out a burner phone. "I cloned your phone as soon as we caught you in Lloyd. Your dad called them and found out about your plans."

My father sits forward, his smirk spreading like a rictus. His eyes are tiny beads. "Doesn't take much to get people's cooperation when you have a pile of cash in one hand and a gun in the other, honey."

I stare at Marcel and Amelie. Amelie glances at me nervously—and then narrows her eyes. "You should have fucking told us you were running from the mob!"

My breath catches in my throat. I can't say she's wrong. But her enormous cowardice and greed still stands out like a monument. "How did they get your address, Amelie?" I demand.

She pales. "What?"

"Your address wasn't in my phone and it's not searchable online. I checked before I left to make sure my dad couldn't track me. Even if they cloned my phone, the only way for them to have your address is if you told them."

My father is laughing again as he watches me put the pieces together. I swallow my tears, not wanting to entertain him further.

"You got it in one, honey," my father chuckles, his tone teasing. "The gun only came out after we got here. They sold you out for deposit money on a house."

I stare at Amelie, all my screaming and crying locked inside.

"Well, I..." she starts.

"The market is very competitive! We would have no chance without this!" Marcel blurts out—and Amelie, still concerned with looking good, snaps at him in French. He goes quiet, glaring at her.

It still hurts. I look away from them in disgust.

My father bends down—chest hitching slightly in pain, but his eyes steady—and stares at me. "You can't get away from me," he rasps. "You're never going to fucking get away from me. And believe me, you're going to pay for this."

I stare back at him, unblinking. I'm not quite sure it's lost yet, but even so, I'll sooner bleed more than shed another tear for his pleasure.

Chase, where are you?

My father chuckles and sits back. "Okay, Benny, call the boys, have them warm up the cars. It's time to go home." Benny obligingly uses the burner phone. He frowns after a moment. "I got no bars."

"That's weird, I had bars a few minutes ago. Okay, go down and tell those bastards in person. I don't want to sit in the cold while the heaters get up to speed." He waves dismissively at Benny, still keeping an eye on me.

"Sure thing, Boss," Benny says, heaving himself out of his seat and heading for the door. He glances at me once, and almost looks guilty.

His hand was on the door handle when an ear-bending crash of metal and glass makes us all jump. It sounds like a car accident—and it happened at the side of the building.

"What the hell was that?" my father demands, splashing liquor as his arms flail in exasperation.

Chase?

My breath goes cold in my chest as I hear a single gunshot. Shouting. Oh no, he doesn't have a gun! But they have guns—will he be okay?

Another crash. Benny opens the door, letting in a blast of cold air that stings my lip, and he runs out, slamming it behind him.

My father pulls out his pistol and aims it at me. "Is that your boyfriend making a mess out there?"

I stare into his eyes defiantly. I want to scare him. And so I lie.

"That's the Sixth Family coming for you, Daddy. They arranged the transport. That man is just one of theirs. I don't even know him."

The horrified reaction from Amelie and Marcel is icing on the cake. "What? You were using our home as a meet-up place for criminals?"

"Why not? You used your home to set up an ambush for me with the Don of New York. And for the record, if you hadn't betrayed me, they would never have come looking for me."

Amelie starts crying. I turn my battered face to smirk at my father—and stare at the barrel of his gun.

"Call them off," he requests.

"How am I supposed to do that? They have all the power. You're the one who fucked up and stepped into their territory without an invitation."

He's never been able to tell when I'm lying. I've survived because of it. He's also drunk.

When the bottle of booze hits the floor and the rest of the contents spill out, he doesn't even notice. His gun wavers.

"All you had to do was let me go," I say quietly, not sure if he's about to shoot me through the face or unfasten me.

"Not a chance." He shoves his gun back in his belt and lumbers for the door. "I'm going to sort this out. Call in some favors. Clean up your mess. Then we're going home, and you're going to face the consequences."

"Wait, what about our money?" Marcel requests, standing up. "You said—"

"Don't, you idiot—" I say too late. My father draws and fires, barely looking, and Marcel falls backwards behind the couch, threads of blood on the wall. Amelie starts sobbing like a siren and dives for him.

My father walks out the door, tucking his gun away and putting on a cheesy grin. What is he really walking into? He's alone and whatever he's preparing for, it's not the situation he'll find.

I don't even look back at Amelie. My feet aren't tied—only my hands behind my back. I heave myself onto my feet, nearly falling over, and run to get my foot in the door before it closes.

I listen frantically over Amelie's screams for my father's footsteps to fade, then nudge the door open and watch him turning the corner, heading toward the back of the building where the racket of the crash came from.

I stumble out and run the other direction, off balance, but as fast as I can. I bang my shoulder turning the corner and nearly lose my stability completely, but I can see daylight from the front stairwell ahead.

I bolt for the last corner—and then a figure steps around it and nearly runs into me.

I stumble back, biting back a scream—and then I'm looking into Chase's amber eyes and sob with relief.

"Oh, my God." He grabs me, hugs me tight, then sees my arms are tied and hurriedly pulls me around the corner. "I was coming to get you. How are your friends?"

"I don't want to talk about it," I gasp into his shoulder as he pulls out a pocket knife and cuts the cords off my wrists. "Let's just get out of here."

He frees my hands and grabs one of them and we run, down the last bit of hallway and down the stairs. It's quiet outside; my heart is pounding, and I wonder if my father is about to come around the corner.

A screech of tires come from the building's driveway. A battered black LTD rockets past, with my father alone at the wheel. We gawk as he fishtails.

"He ran for it," Chase breathes in incredulity. A second later, Benny comes running after the car, waving desperately. The car slows down briefly—but then takes off, leaving Benny in the dust. He just keeps running after it, disappearing from sight.

Chase is laughing. "He fucking ran for it without checking on his guys! I wonder what had him so scared?"

I'm fighting a smile. "Uh, well about that. I kind of told him you worked for the Don of Montreal. He's terrified of the guy."

His eyes widen...and then he lets out a laugh. "Holy shit, you're amazing. Come on, let's get the hell out of here."

I nod and let a smile out. It's like a stone has been lifted off my heart.

We hurry down the street toward the SUV—only to have a tall woman with a silvery braid intercept us. I skid to a stop, heart hammering, but if she has a gun she isn't drawing it.

Chase stops, expression calm. "You saw him rabbit?"

"Yes, he's headed to his own territory. Three of his men are on the way to the hospital once the ambulances get here, and Lucca and the two others have run for it. Thank you for your cooperation." She's so formal, I immediately peg her as a cop of some kind—American, not a local.

"I held up my end. Can we go?" Chase is getting tenser.

"There's just one last thing." And she turns to me, holding out a card. "If you want to be rid of your father, there's a straightforward, legal way to do so. All you have to do is testify against him."

"You mean...you're planning to put him away?" That means no more running!

"Yes, I am. Thanks to Chase's cooperation, we'll pick him up the moment he crosses the border. But putting him in jail is going to take work."

She offers a small smile. "Your testifying could make all the difference."

Chase is gently cradling my hand. We look at each other, and then I look at the cop.

"A man in 301 needs a medic if he's not already dead. He has a bullet wound to the chest. Please take care of it. As for testifying against my father...there are conditions. But we can make a deal." I firmly meet her gaze as I slip her card into my coat pocket.

She nods, texting something into her phone. "Who shot him?"

"My father. I'm hoping that man is the last one he'll ever hurt." The thought of Marcel collapsed and Amelie screaming claws at my heart suddenly.

Sorry, Marcel. I'm partly to blame for this. But the rest was your greed and stupidity. You're a shitty friend, but I hope you don't die.

"I'll make sure he's triaged before those thugs. They'll need the Jaws of Life to peel them out of their cars. Nice job staging that crash," she says to Chase.

"Just took some resourcefulness, and a two-by-four." His smile is tight. "Are we good?"

She nods, stepping aside. "I'll expect a call in a few days then, Miss Lucca."

"Fine." I turn back to Chase. "Let's get cleaned up somewhere."

Chapter 15
Melissa

"I'm so sorry I didn't get to you sooner, sweetheart," Chase says in the hotel room as he helps me out of my clothes. "Are you all right?"

My lip hurts; he has to kiss me on the other side of my mouth so he doesn't aggravate it. "I will be. The knot on my head's probably the worst of it, but I barely even have a headache. Let's just check the damage."

It's not as bad as I expected. I'm sore, but the actual bruises, cuts, and welts aren't remotely hospital-worthy. I've had a lot worse.

He kisses each injury as we uncover it, and leads me to the bathroom in my underwear before almost reverently stripping me. He slips off his turtleneck and draws me a bath, settling me into the hot, perfumed water and leaning on the edge of the bathtub to carefully scrub me down.

My wrists sting where the cords bound them, but there's no permanent damage.

"What happened after I went up to the apartment?" I ask. He already knows about Marcel and Amelie: the betrayal for the money that I could have given them, the stupidity that got Marcel shot—perhaps mortally.

"The FBI agent approached me. She had the apartment watched after following your dad from the border." He gently runs the sudsy sponge down my bare arm. "She offered to help me free you, and I didn't have any options, so I took her up on it."

"You engineered a car crash? How?"

He grins lopsidedly as he slowly and luxuriantly scrubs my back. "I sent one of the FBI agent's rentals into your dad's motor pool with a two-by-four propped against the gas pedal. I bailed before it hit."

"Wow." No wonder it was such a loud crash. "Bet she's not getting her deposit back." His tender caresses with the slightly raspy sponge soothe and arouse me, making the day's trials wash off with the suds.

"Nope, but I doubt she cares. That one is kind of a maverick, and I'm glad. If she went by the book, I'd be in jail and you'd probably still be in your father's hands." He rinses my neck and then presses a soft kiss into it.

"I guess we were all really lucky," I mutter before turning my head to offer him my mouth.

We're finally alone, in private, behind locked doors, not hunted...and I'm thirsty to take advantage. There's nothing to stop us anymore. And we both know it. I can see it in the gleam in his eyes.

The bath and tending of my wounds mixes with more teasing and caressing, the sponge circling over my breasts until my nipples ache to be sucked, sweeping between my thighs and ass cheeks like a big, rough tongue. By the time he lifts me, rinsed and dripping, from the water to carry me to the purple-upholstered bed, I'm trembling and panting for air.

He lays me down and practically tears off the rest of his clothes. His massive cock bounds up against his muscular belly; I stare at it for a short time before he throws himself over me and starts covering me with kisses.

He explores every part of my body with his hands and mouth, his tongue tracing over my hipbone, his mouth leaving hickeys up my spine, his teeth scraping softly against my neck as his hands knead my bare breasts. When he finally starts suckling at my nipples again, I almost climax. My pussy clenches, aching with emptiness, my thighs rubbing together with lust and frustration as the nipple play draws me to the brink but won't push me over.

"I need you inside of me," I gasp out, and when he looks up at me his golden-brown eyes are full of passion. Then he gently parts my thighs and settles between them, teasing the head of his cock between my slick folds. His hand settles over my pussy again, and he stimulates me with delicate strokes as he enters with almost maddening tardiness.

When he finally thrusts deep into me, I'm humming with desire, so desperately aroused that I go up on my heels and push back eagerly as the unfamiliar bulk of his cock slides in.

"Ohh!" he gasps, muscles going taut and back arching as he presses me into the mattress. His cock is hot and sleek inside of me, throbbing in time to his heart pounding against my breasts.

"Oh, God," Chase groans into my shoulder, slowly churning his thick organ inside my aching, tingling flesh. My pussy tightens around him, and he moans again, head tilting back and lips parted. "Oh, so good."

He trembles above me, his struggle for self-control driving me even wilder. His erection stretches me in ways that intensify the pleasure of his fingers teasing my clit; his hand quivers as he strokes me, but never wavers.

He starts to thrust slowly, his movements loving, even as his fingers tease me closer to climax. I croon softly each time he sinks in deep, my breath shuddering and growing more shallow as my muscles tighten.

Knowing what's coming, knowing that ecstasy, I'm all the more eager to feel it again. And he's getting me there, patient and measured, until I'm begging for it. "Oh, yes, just like that," I gasp out. "Don't stop!"

My whole body shakes; every stroke of his finger and cock feels better than the last. I cling to his heaving shoulders and grind eagerly against him; he shouts with pleasure and speeds his movements while I writhe and sob under him.

And suddenly his swirling finger makes the ultimate stroke, and my body takes off, pleasure roaring through me while I thrash helplessly.

He keeps fingering me until my screams of bliss drop down to satisfied coos...and only then does he draw his hand away and take hold of my hips.

The bed shakes under us, springs creaking as he thrusts faster and harder. Our bellies clap together; bliss rocks through me and I grab his magnificent ass and raise my hips to meet him.

Satisfaction has transformed him; he moves tirelessly, every muscle taut, breath shuddering and erratic as he moves faster.

I'm building toward climax again, his insistent fucking stimulating me in new ways as my gasps and moans mix with his. I never thought sex could feel this good; now I revel in it. It's my rebellion. It's my revenge. It's paradise. Watching his face, strained but idyllic, lips parted, eyes closed, stokes my desire up further. He speeds up again, growing rougher, and I'm too turned on to feel anything but hunger for the next thrust.

"Do it, do it, do it," I sob shamelessly, feeling his ass flex and tremble under my hands as his hot shaft pounds into me. My pussy tightens around him hungrily, more and more...and then another wave of contractions makes me screech and mill on his cock.

He stiffens and then shouts again, and I feel his member jump and jolt inside me as he thrusts as deep as he can. His deep-voiced pants and grunts echo off the walls as his days of waiting end; as I watch his ecstasy drive him wild.

It passes, and he settles over me softly, still buried inside me. "So good," he whispers reverently as he kisses my neck.

I slide my hands up his back and he shivers with pleasure; I stroke my hands over his shorn hair and he lays his head on my shoulder, relaxing entirely.

It's done. And with someone that I like and want to be with.

My father would be furious.

Good.

"I want more when we wake up," I whisper as he rolls us over so I can fall asleep on his chest.

"Gladly," he purrs. "As much as you want."

As I drift off, I know that's going to be a lot. Every night. For the rest of our lives, if we can keep it together.

And I'm pretty confident that we can as I slip into dreamland. We're good together...and all things considered, our good fortune has been incredible.

Chapter 16
Alan

We've been in this hotel room for two days, ordering room service and retiring to the Jacuzzi on the enclosed balcony when the maid comes in to straighten up. Melissa is healing; I'm exhausting from demonstrating every sex position she shows interest in.
The staff thinks we're newlyweds and giggle about us in French, which I listen in on while pretending obliviousness. Their rumors are cute and innocent and much kinder than the truth. They would never have known that I met the love of my life less than a week ago in the trunk of a mobster's car.
I've been out for condoms twice in as many days. Despite my size, we haven't needed lube. She's sleeping it off as I dry from my shower and sit down in a towel to check the news on my laptop. Life is good. I'm in love with a

beautiful, amazing woman who wants to stay, we're rolling in currency, and the FBI is off my ass and her father is off of hers.

Maybe it's not exactly a happy ending. We've made a mess in the Sixth Family's town, and that's a good way to wear out your welcome. We're planning to pick up my truck and go to California for the winter as soon as we get word that Lucca and his enforcers have been rounded up.

After that, we'll need to stay out of Montreal and New York for a while—and Chicago, where her creep "fiancé" is from. That's fine. There's a whole continent we can roam together.

My new friend at the Bureau has news for me, sent in an encrypted email. It's actually pretty cool to have a connection on the right side of the law. When I open the email and read through it, alarm goes through me, and I just sit there for a while.

The good news:

Marcel Delacroix survived and is expected to make a full recovery. He woke up late last night and is lucid. He and his wife are cooperating with Montreal police in investigating the shooting.

Several of Lucca's lieutenants have now surrendered or been arrested, along with Melissa's brothers. You should have no trouble returning to the States with Melissa.

The bad news:

Regrettably, there will now be no trial. Gianni Lucca was shot by an assassin disguised as a border guard. The hired gun was heard to say the Don of Montreal sends his regards.

Lucca was rushed to emergency surgery and was on life support until half an hour ago. Although his men will be prosecuted for lesser crimes, we likely will not need Melissa's testimony. On the other hand, she needs no longer fear her father.

Good luck out there!

I turn off the computer, closing it up and unplugging it. Then I quietly start packing all of our stuff. It's still before checkout time.

Melissa rolls over and blinks at me sleepily. "What is it?" she mumbles.

"No urgent situation, sweetheart, but we need to get out of Montreal. Your family caused a dust-up here and the local Family is pissed. They probably won't blame us for anything, but I feel like we should give them space."

I'm not telling her yet that her father is dead; we don't have time to sit and process that.

"That sounds pretty somber. I'm still a Lucca, after all. They have no idea I was fleeing from him." She stays calm and gets up, going for her suitcase and a fresh change of clothes.

The guy behind the desk looks oddly familiar, watching us with piercing dark eyes as we check out. I'm tired, fucked out, and in a hurry; I don't even think about it until later, when we're crossing over the border to pick up my truck.

An assassin disguised as a border guard.

"Oh shit," I mutter, going cold. I remember him from last time. The one who stared at us while the other did the talking.

"What is it?" she asks hurriedly, worry in her voice as she turns to me.

"I think we were being watched at the hotel," I say as delicately as I can. "All the better we left."

I end up telling Melissa about her father that night, once we have my truck from Paulie. We're parked in a Walmart parking lot next to some campers and sitting in the warm little cabin while I hold her hands.

"Do they know who did it?" she questions breathlessly, face pale as she struggles to process the news.

"No idea. Might be someone from the Sixth Family, might be someone they hired. Between the bullets, the crash, and the delay getting to surgery, your dad didn't make it."

She closes her eyes and lies back against the pillows at the head of the bed, sighing softly and smoothing the silk of her pink negligee over her belly. My eyes trace the movement and my cock starts firming up despite the solemn conversation.

"Good," she says quietly. Tears of relief run down her cheeks. "If he's departed, I really am free."

I snuggle next to her and wrap my arms around her.

"Yeah," I comfort her as I lean in to kiss her tears away. "You are. And I'm going to make sure we both stay that way."

Epilogue
Carolyn

"According to this report, Alan Chase and Melissa Lucca disappeared and may currently be 'guests' of the Sixth Family. Or deceased after having been guests." Derek Daniels leans over his desk at me, his dark beard jutting aggressively.
"That is correct, sir." I'm composed as I sit in one of my best dark wool suits across from him. None of this ended ideally...but I'm still making a name for myself against Daniels' wishes, and it's driving him crazy.
He flaps the pages against his desktop. "Meanwhile, Gianni Lucca was murdered by a presumed Sixth Family assassin for his invading their territory? Simultaneously, Enzo Capurro was murdered by a second mysterious man in Chicago? Wasn't he about to marry Melissa Lucca?"

I nod. "Yes, sir, as it states in the report."
"That's a great jumble and other people will deal with." He drops the papers on his desk in a gesture of determination. "Go back to your list. Your first guy may be in deep shit in Montreal, but there are four others who need to be apprehended."
I stare in dismay before making my expression neutral again. "Of course, sir. I can get back on the road after this weekend."
"Tomorrow. I'll send a courier with plane tickets." Just the most minuscule hint of a smirk on his lips at my discomfort.
"Yes, sir," I reply stiffly, and he waves me out.
"You don't even stay home for more than a night?" Misty, one of my roommates, asks in incredulity an hour later. She's a statuesque Brazilian woman who works for a boutique internet company.
"I know it's been my turn to cook for like, a week." I smile regretfully as I sit on my bed packing.
She leans against my doorway and folds her arms. "That Daniels guy is a dick. I'm glad you never slept with him."
"Yeah, me too, but half the shit he does to me is because I didn't. Welcome to sexism." I scoff. "Anyway, I'm not giving up my v-card to some married creep."
"Good call. And don't worry about the cooking. Let's order a pizza and watch some bad science fiction instead." Her nose wrinkles mischievously.
"You pick the movie, I'll order the pizza. I just got a bonus!" It came through official channels, but not from Daniels. He doesn't give a damn I flushed Lucca into an

FBI trap I helped lay, because dead mobsters don't get him any glory.

He wouldn't help Alan Chase save Melissa, either. And he'd be furious to know I let them escape.

Me, I'm just irritated. There are a lot worse people than Alan Chase, and I want to focus on putting them away where they can't hurt anyone else. Instead, I'm right back where I started—and I'm here half-intentionally.

Yet I can say that I did the right thing.

I log onto my laptop to order the pizza, too tired to deal with another phone call. I see a new email and open my inbox idly—only to see a strange email from a bulk address.

Well done, Special Agent.

It is inopportune you did not make a name for yourself with the capture of Gianni Lucca. His reach was too great to ever have seen a day in jail. His death was required.

It is regrettable as well that Alan Chase must remain free. But men of conscience are uncommon on either side of the law. Satisfy yourself by knowing Melissa Lucca—soon to be Melissa Chase—will now thrive, out of the reach of her father or ex-fiancé.

Your conscience is greater than your ambition. If you continue to pay attention to me, I will do everything to correct that. I will be in contact soon. There are some imperative things you need to know about your next assignment.

I stare at the words then send a reply.

Who are you?

I hit send and wait breathlessly...only for the email to bounce back as undeliverable.

"Damn it!" I snap, furious and disgusted with my powerlessness.

"Something wrong?" Misty sticks her head back in. "I'm putting on Plan 9 From Outer Space, it's quite funny."

"Nothing. Good. Just having some trouble with the website." I mumble distractedly as I start entering the order.

"Oh. There's about a billion to choose from now, it's Brooklyn. Come out when you're done, okay?"

"Of course." I finish ordering and am getting my debit card to pay when I notice a credit for one hundred dollars entered under two minutes ago. It's a gift.

But from whom?

I check the notes on the gift card as soon as I finalize the order—and I stop, a weird thrill running through me. A note is attached to the gift card.

Call me Prometheus.

The End

ALL RIGHTS RESERVED. No part of this publication may be reproduced or transmitted in any form whatsoever, electronic, or mechanical, including photocopying, recording, or by any informational storage or retrieval system without express written, dated and signed permission from the author.

DISCLAIMER AND/OR LEGAL NOTICES: Every effort has been made to accurately represent this book and it's potential. Results vary with every individual, and your results may or may not be different from those depicted. No promises, guarantees or warranties, whether stated or implied, have been made that you will produce any specific result from this book. Your efforts are individual and unique, and may vary from those shown. Your success depends on your efforts, background and motivation.

The material in this publication is provided for educational and informational purposes only and is not intended as medical advice. The information contained in this book should not be used to diagnose or treat any illness, metabolic disorder, disease or health problem. Always consult your physician or health care provider before beginning any nutrition or exercise program. Use of the programs, advice, and information contained in this book is at the sole choice and risk of the reader.

www.ingramcontent.com/pod-product-compliance
Lightning Source LLC
LaVergne TN
LVHW011717060526
838200LV00051B/2923